Really Beautiful Company

Really Beautiful Company

Traditional Singers and Musicians of Gloucestershire

Carol Davies

Matador
9 Priory Business Park,
Wistow Road, Kibworth Beauchamp,
Leicestershire. LE8 0RX
Tel: 0116 279 2299
Email: books@troubador.co.uk
Web: www.troubador.co.uk/matador
Twitter: @matadorbooks

ISBN 9781788035996

British Library Cataloguing in Publication Data.
A catalogue record for this book is available from the British Library.

Printed and bound by CPI Group (UK) Ltd, Croydon, CR0 4YY
Typeset in 11pt Aldine401 BT by Troubador Publishing Ltd, Leicester, UK

Matador is an imprint of Troubador Publishing Ltd

To my husband, Gwilym, for his expertise in song collecting and his support while I have been researching this book

CONTENTS

PREFACE

Do we all have singing ancestors? In the days before mass media, the only music that most people would have heard would have that made by themselves, their friends or their family. What do we know of these singers and musicians? What songs have people sung in Gloucestershire to cheer themselves up on cold winter nights? When there was no television or radio or ipods what songs did farming folk enjoy at Harvest Homes and when they were out on the hills looking after Cotswold sheep? What amused people when they were relegated to the workhouse? What songs are still sung that have been handed down through the generations?

Over the years songs and tunes passed down through friends and family have entertained in towns and villages. We only know about this rich heritage of songs and music through the tireless efforts of song collectors such as Cecil Sharp and the musician, Percy Grainger, who sought them out. The National Lottery funded project 'The Single Gloucester' has given us the opportunity to explore this rich heritage of Gloucestershire and they are now available for all to see on the website www.glostrad.com, but what about the people who sang and played them? During the course of my research for this project I have come to respect and marvel at the traditional singers and musicians of Gloucestershire. This book looks at the character of local singers in Gloucestershire – who were they? What did they do? How did they live? What can we learn about the social conditions at the time various songs were sung?

There are hundreds of songs and tunes from Gloucestershire on the www.glostrad.com website and in this book I have tried to choose a representative sample of the singers and musicians that we have discovered from the area. This book aims to pull together the major themes of life in Gloucestershire and the people who lived there. There are many further interesting singers and musicians on the website and others will no doubt enjoy exploring there. For those wishing to know more about a singer or the places mentioned, the appendices contain a more comprehensive list of songs collected from each of the singers in this book and the places where they lived.

One might think that Gloucestershire labourers mainly living in poor conditions would sing songs of complaint about their plight, but in fact the reverse is true. They glorified their rural life by singing songs such as "We shepherds are the best of men" or "There's none can lead a jollier life than Jim the Carter's Lad". They also sang of love, war, lords and ladies, humour and so on.

This book will be of interest to anyone who wants to find out more about the social context of Gloucestershire rural singers, social history in Gloucestershire, or family history. In writing this book my thanks go to the many people who have contributed to the website, but especially to the trustees of Gloucestershire Traditions, and to my husband, Gwilym, for his expertise on song collecting and patience in editing my words. Also to my publishers and the following who have contributed their knowledge: Richard Sermon about singers from Tewkesbury, Keith Chandler for information on the morris dance musicians of Sherborne and the family history researchers and families of the singers who have been so helpful in my research.

This is not a book about songs but about the people who sang them. One of Percy Grainger's singers described her time singing to him as 'Really Beautiful Company' and I hope you find the same here.

Carol Davies
Gloucestershire 2017

1

PLACES

Sherborne

SINGERS AND MUSICIANS IN SHERBORNE – A TYPICAL COTSWOLD VILLAGE

Fig. 1

Sherborne is a typical small Gloucestershire village with a well-documented history which has produced a good number of musicians, dancers and singers and so is a great example of a place where various families have interacted on the artistic level, with regard to songs, dances, music and customs. Sherborne provides us with a microcosm of a community of traditional performers.

The picture of the village that emerges throughout the 19th century is one of a close-knit community of inter-related families on low incomes, with several generations living together in crowded conditions in what were then quite humble Cotswold dwellings. Elders are frequently listed as paupers and children were sent out to work at an early age. Work was almost exclusively agriculture and social life revolved around common interests of music, song, dance and mumming. As there is no record of a public house in the village, one can assume that the social interaction was house-to-house. The following chapter studies five Sherborne families in particular, namely the Buntings, the Simpsons, the Hopkins, the Hoopers and the Pitts, members of whom played, danced, sang or acted as mummers, all living in close proximity and in some cases inter-married.

THE VILLAGE

Fig. 2. The picturesquely named Ash Hole Road in Sherborne, home to many of the traditional singers and musicians

In Gloucestershire much of the countryside was owned by large estates and most people who lived in the villages worked on the estates, usually on the land. According to the 1841 Census, 17.4 % of the population in Gloucestershire were engaged in agriculture of whom 79% were agricultural labourers. Of the employed people in Gloucestershire 36% were engaged in commerce, trade and manufacture, 17.3% were employed as domestic servants and 15.1 % were farmers or graziers. These are the principal employments that we find in Sherborne.

Central to the social structure of the village was, and still is to some extent, the large manor and estate of Sherborne House, which was built for Thomas Dutton after he bought the manor of Sherborne in 1551. The house and estate supplied employment for a high proportion of the inhabitants of the village, but many were employed in any one of the large farms clustered around the village.

Fig. 3. Sherborne House

By 1841 Sherborne village had a population of 637, of whom 209 were in employment. The majority were employed as agricultural labourers – 109 in all, working for six tenant farmers. Eight were employed in associated trades: 3 grooms, 4 gamekeepers and 1 gardener supervised by 1 park keeper and 2 bailiffs.

The building trade was also a big employer. In 1841 Sherborne had no less than 15 carpenters, 2 joiners, 1 plumber, 7 stone masons, 1 slater and 4 sawyers. The village also had a number of essential tradesmen: a miller, a blacksmith, a baker, 2 shoemakers, a draper, a pig dealer and 2 wheelwrights.

Noticeably lacking were any professional people such as a doctor who would presumably have to be visited in the nearby town of Northleach. This spread of occupations continued in Sherborne for many years.

It is clear that traditional song and music thrived in the village as evidenced by the several collectors who came there looking for traditional songs and tunes and it was among the agricultural community that they found them.

SHERBORNE SINGERS

One of the agricultural labourers on the estate, **Thomas Bunting**, sang songs to the song collector James Madison Carpenter sometime around 1930. Some of his songs had been learned from his father sixty years previously and are representative of the country singers' repertoire of the time: the ballad Barbara Allen, the well-known song *Johnny's So Long at the Fair,* the nonsense song *Old Woman Tossed Up,* and courting songs *The American Stranger (The Green Mossy Banks of the Lea), The Pretty Ploughboy* and *Seventeen come Sunday*. Like other estates, Sherborne employed gamekeepers and another of Thomas' songs, which he learnt from his father James, was the poaching song *While Gamekeepers Lie Sleeping*. In fact, the Bunting family provided three generations of gamekeepers for Sherborne as Carpenter stated that Thomas, his father James and his grandfather William all worked as gamekeepers and lived all their lives in Sherborne.

Thomas Bunting came from a long line of Sherborne residents. His grandparents, William, born 1812 and Hannah, lived their lives in Sherborne and died in 1873 and 1891 respectively. Their son James was born 1832. In 1858 James married Mary and they had 9 children, including Thomas, born in 1862. Living in the country the younger members of the family supported the elderly relatives and William was described in the 1891 census as supported by his son and grandson and died shortly afterwards. James may have been a morris dancer and lived until 1908. There are records of a Thomas Bunting living in the Chipping Norton area in the 20th century.

An important musical family and source of songs was the Pitts family and especially **Thomas Pitts**, born 1855, who was

also a member of the Sherborne morris dance side. With the Pitts' musical background, it was logical that folk music collectors would visit them, particularly Thomas and his son Charles. In 1934, Thomas came to the attention of local folk song collector Harry Albino and the then young morris dancer and researcher Russell Wortley.[1] Thomas was then 79 years old and living in Eastleach. He sang 2 songs to Albino, namely *Fair Young Damsel* (also known as *The Box on her Head*) and *Jim The Carter's Lad*. He also apparently sang the morris tunes *Bonnets [so] Blue* and *Green Garters*. At the same time, Albino took some important photographs of Thomas who talked to him about his pipe and tabor playing and demonstrated the tabor technique with a small tambourine.

Figs. 4 & 5. Thomas Pitts.
Photos by H. H. Albino
Courtesy Gloucestershire
Archives

Unfortunately, the great English song collector Cecil Sharp never met Thomas to ask him about the Sherborne Morris, presumably because Thomas was not living in Sherborne at the time.

Previously the song collector Alfred Williams had visited Thomas Pitts' wife, Esther, who sang him *Early in the Morning* (also known as *South Carolina is a Sultry Clime*), a song that must have come over to England with the black-faced minstrel tradition. It is a pity that Williams did not ask Thomas for songs at the same time.

Albino subsequently visited Thomas' son, **Charles Pitts**, on 3 October 1935 who sang further traditional songs, mainly dealing with the countryside. Like his father, he sang *The Fair Young Damsel* and *Jim The Carter Lad* and also added *It's Of A Comely Young Lady Fair* or *Phoebe and the Dark-eyed Sailor* (usually known as *The Dark-Eyed Sailor*). Albino returned to visit Charles Pitts a couple of months later and collected a version of *We're All Jolly Fellows That Follow the Plough*. We therefore have a good example of a son carrying on his father's tradition.

As noted above, the collector Russell Wortley visited Thomas before WWII and then in 1956 he visited Charles, then aged 78 and living in Brize Norton. Charles played to him some dance tunes: *The Rose Tree, the Keel Row. Bonnets So Blue*, a march and a hornpipe. Wortley also interviewed Charles' aunt Mrs (Sarah) Drinkwater, who talked about country dances. Several inhabitants of Sherborne village went in for dance and supported the Sherborne morris dance side. Thomas's father, Richard, born 1824, was not a morris man but told folk dance collector Clive Carey about 1913 that he remembered morris dancers in Sherborne named Hedges, Hawker, Lambert and two brothers Kent, one called John. He also recalled a Mr Simpson as playing music on the 'whistle and dub' (pipe and tabor) for the morris dancing, almost certainly Jim "The Laddie" Simpson/MacDonald referred to below. The village gave rise to a number of pipe and tabor players. At one time before the mid-19th century, pipe and tabor was the exclusive instrument for Cotswold morris dancing and it seems that its use lingered on in Sherborne longer than elsewhere as Thomas Pitts was the last surviving traditional pipe and tabor. The pipe and tabor is a three holed pipe which can be held in one hand, leaving the other hand free to play the tabor drum. It is also known as the 'whittle and drum'.

The Pitts family were agricultural workers who were long-time residents of the village of Sherborne. The family of Thomas Pitts' grandfather, also called Thomas, had lived in Great Barrington for several generations but moved into Sherborne when he married Mary Dodge from Sherborne, in Sherborne on 8 November 1803. Their son Richard, Thomas' father, was born in 1823 and by 1841, still in Sherborne, the family had acquired 2 more sons, Thomas and George. Richard married Caroline Hall from Maugersbury, near Stow-on-the-Wold, in 1849. Thomas' parents, described as paupers, were living with the couple in 1851 and Richard was working on the land as was his grandfather.

Richard and Caroline continued the family tradition of naming their children after their parents and so their son, Thomas, was baptised in 1855 in Sherborne. As well as Thomas, the couple had other children, namely Mary (born 1853), John (born c1859), William (born c1860), Sarah (born c1867) and Eliza (born c1869), all born in Sherborne. By 1861 we find the family still in Sherborne, although grandfather Thomas had died and Mary was a widow. Richard continued to work as an agricultural labourer and 3 of his sons, Thomas, John and William as ploughboys. Also living with them was Caroline's father, described as a pauper.

Caroline died sometime before 1881 when Richard was a widower, still living in Sherborne and working as an agricultural labourer with his sons, John, a carrier, William, an

Fig. 6. Richard Pitts at his garden gate, 1912. Photo taken by Lillian Tremaine, a resident of Sherborne, one year prior to his death.[2]

agricultural labourer, and daughter, Sarah. Sarah then married Frederick Drinkwater, an agricultural labourer from Brize Norton, and by 1891 the couple were living with Richard in Sherborne with their son, Charles Frank Drinkwater born about 1888. Frederick, like Richard, was working as an agricultural labourer.

By 1911 Richard was living at No 54 Sherborne with Frederick and Sarah, the former working as a gardener. Sarah was a grocer and confectioner, their son Charles was by then a cowman and they had another son, John, at school. Another child died young.

Figs. 7–9. No 54 Sherborne now

It is interesting to note that the house which then was probably a modest Cotswold cottage with several generations of the family living in the same house, is now a Grade II listed Cotswold stone building in Sherborne.

Meanwhile in 1876, Richard and Caroline's son Thomas, the singer, had married Esther Jackson, also from Sherborne, and shortly afterwards had a son, William Richard, followed in 1878 by another son, Charles Edwin Pitts. In 1881 they were still living in Sherborne where Thomas was working as an oxman. They had another son, James, born that year. In 1883 they had a daughter, Sarah Ann, born in Coln St Aldwyns, followed by a son, Frederick Thomas born in 1886 on Cocklebarrow Farm, Aldsworth and another daughter, Eliza, born in Eastleach in 1887, so it can be seen that the family moved around, probably from farm to farm, but by 1891 they back in Sherborne where Thomas was working as a carter and agricultural labourer. His two sons, William and Charles, were also agricultural labourers and his other children, James and Sarah were still at school. That same year they had another daughter, Florence Mary E. Pitts, born on Aston Farm, Gloucestershire, possibly in Shipton–under-Wychwood. By 1901 the family had moved to The Downs, Shipton-under-Wychwood, Oxfordshire where Thomas was working as a carter on a farm. His son, Frederick, was an under carter on a farm and his daughters Eliza and Florence were the only other two children still at home. Thomas's son, Charles, had moved away from home and was by then working as a carter on a farm in Lyneham, Oxfordshire. In 1911 Thomas and Esther were living in Eastleach Turville, Lechlade with their son, Frederick, aged 24 who was unmarried. Thomas and Frederick were both working as farm labourers. Richard Pitts died in 1913, Esther in 1925, Thomas in 1940, both of the latter being buried in Eastleach.

The progression of Thomas' life and work is untypical as

unlike many Sherborne families that lived all their lives in the village, Thomas and Esther frequently moved from place to place within a small area. Nevertheless, in his younger days, Thomas had joined the Sherborne Morris and had learnt the art of the pipe and tabor.

Thomas and Esther's son, Charles, married Edith Agnes Lowe in 1904. Edith was from Glympton, Oxfordshire, the daughter of James Lowe, an agricultural labourer. She had previously worked as a housekeeper to her father in Cassington, Oxfordshire. In 1901 Edith had been living in one of three houses called 'sheephouse' in Eastleach Martin with her sister, Alice, and Alice's husband who was a shepherd, and their family. She already had a daughter, Muriel Harriet M. Lowe, born out of wedlock in 1898 and very shortly after her marriage to Charles Pitts she had a son, Walter Charles Lowe, stated to be illegitimate in the 1911 census record. Charles and Edith had a son, Arthur Frederick J Pitts in 1906 (his second name was given as Francis in the 1911 census but on his death in Swindon in 1988 his name was also given as Arthur Frederick). In 1911 Charles and Edith were living on Lechlade Downs, Lechlade where Charles was working as a carter. They had two further daughters, Flora Esther born 1908 and Kathleen Annie born about 1910. Charles Pitts died in 1956 in Oxfordshire.

Another Sherborne singer was **George Hicks.** We know little about George except that the song collector Alfred Williams collected two songs from **William Avery** in Aldsworth between 1913 and 1916, who had learnt songs from George. The songs collected were *Leather Breeches* and *The Ploughman*. About *Leather Breeches* he stated 'This old song was popular in Gloucestershire between Tetbury and Burford. I have not heard it south of the Thames though no doubt it was sung there formerly.' He also said that 'This was sung for many years by George Hicks of Aldsworth, formerly of Sherborne, an old Morris dancer.' The links between the Avery and Hicks family were very close as also living with William Avery's family in 1911 was Emma Hicks, a laundress aged 66 who was the widow of singer George Hicks.

More Sherborne Morris Musicians

By the 19th century the Cotswolds were one of the principal areas for morris dancing in England and the Sherborne morris dancers were considered to be one of the top morris sides of the area. The fiddle player **William Hathaway**, born at Lower Swell on 3 May 1841, described Sherborne as *'a desperate Morris place,'* while the collector Cecil Sharp claimed to have *'repeatedly heard other Morris men speak in similar terms, [and] ..... that the Sherborne men must at one time have held a leading position among the Morris dancers in that part of the country.'* [3]

The major source of information about the Sherborne Morris for collectors, particularly Cecil Sharp, was **George Simpson**, born 1848. Sharp had been given George Simpson's name when he visited the fiddler John Mason in Stow on the Wold in 1907. George was the son of an agricultural labourer, William Simpson, who was born in 1803 and his wife, Hannah Simpson née Paish, born 1818. Both his father, William, and grandfather, John, lived in Sherborne. George's trade was land measuring, the same as the pipe and tabor player, William Hooper (see below), and carpentering. Before Sharp met Simpson, Mrs. Hobbs, who did a lot of exploratory work in the Cotswolds, went to see Mrs. James, widow of the man who taught Simpson. Mrs James regarded the village of Fieldtown as Sherborne's greatest rivals. Sharp also saw Taylor, a pupil of Simpsons, but they all agreed in Sherborne that Simpson was the best and that he could whistle the tunes. In July 1908 George was living in the village of Upton, near Didcot in

Berkshire, where Cecil Sharp visited him and Sharp returned to visit him again on 5, 17, 24 and 31 March 1910. Simpson was subsequently visited in 1913 by the song collector Clive Carey who said he was a bailiff on a farm, but he died shortly afterwards from cancer. George's younger brother James was visited by the Travelling Morrice on 26 June 1938 when living in retirement at Battledown, Cheltenham. Both George and James had danced for the Sherborne morris but both left and joined the police force in Cheltenham. The folk song collector Fred Hamer said they changed their name (when they joined the police), for some reason now forgotten.

George Simpson told Sharp that the dancers at Sherborne used to dance for three weeks on and off at Whitsuntide – he stated that that was the regular outing for the year except for special fêtes. They used to dance for miles around. At Sherborne they always danced on Whit Tuesday and according to a relative of musician Thomas Pitts *'they used to have a quite a bit of fun'*. The side broke up about 1883 but morris dancing was revived in Sherborne for a short time in the mid 1970s and there is a visiting Sherborne morris side these days. Nowadays morris teams from all over the country visit the village to dance there and the dances from Sherborne are incorporated into many Cotswold morris dance sides' repertoires.

Fig. 10. Pipe and tabor player playing for morris dancing

The earliest Sherborne morris musician that we know of was a fiddle player called **Bradshaw** born c1690. There is a record of him being paid by the Dutton family of Sherborne house in 1710.

However, playing the fiddle for morris was not typical at that time as the main instrument to accompany morris dancing was the pipe and tabor.

George Simpson said that **William Harper** of Sherborne used to play whittle and dub (pipe and tabor) and that "Jim the Laddy" **James Simpson/McDonald** (1811-1856) was another pipe and taborer. Other pipe and tabor players in Sherborne were **James Hopkins** (born 1820), **William Hooper** (1836-1927) and **Thomas Pitts** (1855-1940) (see above). Thus Sherborne had a solid tradition of pipe and tabor playing.

James Simpson/McDonald was born James McDonald in Edinburgh on 22 March 1811, probably the child of Alexander McDonald and Jane McKillop, born in Quebec. By 1841 Jane and her son James had moved to Sherborne where they had taken on the surname of Simpson. In that year, Jane was 65 years old and living with them was Thomas Simpson aged 88 an agricultural labourer. It is unknown whether Thomas was Jane's husband or father-in-law, but nevertheless Jane and her son James had taken on his name. Nor is it clear what relationship there is between these Simpsons and the family of George Simpson described above.

James married Priscilla, from Eastleach, and the couple went on to have several children, Sarah (born 1838), Thomas (born 1840), William (born 1844, died 1850), Elizabeth (born 1849), Mary (born 1850) and Rebecca (born 1851). In 1851, James' mother was living with them but described as a pauper. At least one of his children, Thomas, was working on the land at the age of 11.

James presumably took up the pipe and tabor on moving to Sherborne, but died in 1856 in colourful circumstances. In June of that year Jim was playing for the Northleach Morris Men who were doing a tour of the Whitsuntide club feasts. At Bourton-on-the-Water, he became *'so Drunk that He died from the Efects of it'*. On Thursday, June 12th (1856), an inquest was held at a pub called the New Inn, on the body of James Simson [*sic*], of Sherborne; the account continues *"it appears the deceased left home on the Monday previous, as one of a party of morrice dancers proceeding to Stow club, stayed there until the Tuesday night, and when on his way home (alone) he called at the New Inn, in this village, where a party had that day dined, and were spending the evening together. The deceased insisted on joining them, and as drink was to be had without stint, he drank in a short space of time so much that he was obliged to be removed to an apartment, in which he was comfortably laid and covered for the night; every care was taken of him, and the landlady, the last thing, saw him asleep, and left him safe. The following morning, about 9 o'clock, he was found in an uneasy state. Medical assistance was sent for, but before the doctor arrived he had ceased to breath [sic]. Verdict – Died from excess of drink."* [4]. The Northleach Morris ceased dancing soon after this, perhaps for the lack of a musician. Some time afterwards, his pipe came to the possession of Charles Benfield (1841-1929) of Bould, who was musician for the Bledington Morris. Benfield may have played the pipe, but his main morris instrument was the fiddle.

After James' death, his widow, Priscilla, continued to live in Sherborne with her daughter Rebecca and James' mother, Jane, doing field work but by 1871 she was a pauper living on her own. She continued to live in Sherborne on her own until her death in 1892 in the Northleach registration district.

Another pipe and tabor player, **James Hopkins**, was from a long-established Sherborne family. **James'** grandfather, Joseph, a widower, married Jane Bunting in Sherborne in 1787. Jane was from the local Bunting musical family – see above. Their son, also called Joseph, was born about 1788 and married Hannah. Their son, James, was born in about 1820 and another brother, George, was born in 1825 but died at the age of 3. Another possible brother was William Hopkins who died aged 14 in 1828 and possibly Charles Hopkins, born

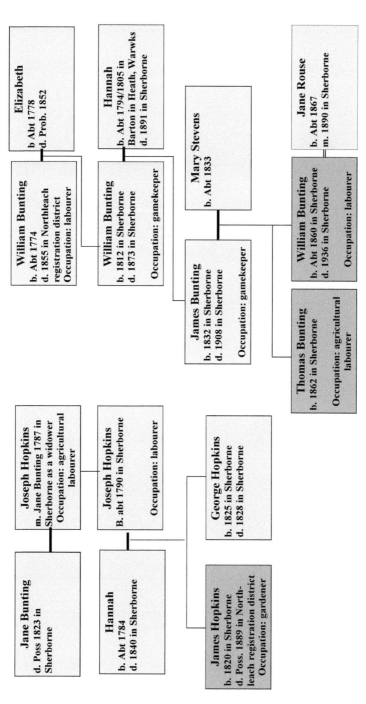

Fig. 11. Family tree for James Hopkins and Thomas and William Bunting

about 1821, who in 1841 was working as a servant for farmer Eli Gillett at Woeful Lake Farm, Sherborne, a large 18th-century stone farm-house. [5]

James' mother, Hannah, died in Sherborne in 1840 and by 1841 James was an agricultural labourer living in Sherborne with his widowed father, Joseph, then aged 50. The Hopkins family lived very near another musical family, the Buntings and as we have seen James' grandmother was née Bunting. Living next door to James and Joseph in 1841 were William and Hannah Bunting, then aged 25 and 35 respectively, with their eight-year old son James and another boy called John Clarke aged 12 who was not from Gloucestershire. Five doors away in 1841 were another Bunting family, Thomas, aged 40, an agricultural labourer, and Mary, aged 30, with their year-old daughter Elizabeth, the aunt and uncle of the singer Thomas Bunting.

By 1851 James and his father were still living in Sherborne, James as a gardener and Joseph an agricultural labourer and ten years later, the two were still living in the village. It is unclear what happened to James after 1871 but a James Hopkins aged 72 died and was buried in the Northleach registration district in 1889.

Another pipe and tabor player for the Sherborne morris, **William Hooper,** came from a long line of established Sherborne families. His grandfather Robert (c1769-1845) was an agricultural labourer in Sherborne. Robert's son David married Jane and they went on to have 12 children, including William, born in 1836. William, David and several other sons were sawyers. Jane died in 1853 and David continued to live with his son William. By 1861, the family was still there. At this time William and his father were described as land measurers (surveyors), a trade in which he was employed into his 70s. William's sister Hannah was their housekeeper while their 12-year old brother Henry had become a sawyer like his father and brothers.

On 23 June 1866 William married Emily Kilby in Upper

Slaughter. Emily's father, Richard Kilby, was a bailiff, a responsible position on an estate. William and Emily had 3 children born in quick succession, Sarah Jane, Mary Annice and Henry Edwin, all born around 1867-1869. Although William had a job which was probably a cut above the average labourer's, in 1871 his 9 year old son was nevertheless working as a ploughboy. By 1881 William and Emily were still living in Sherborne and had another 5 sons and another daughter – in all they had a total of seven sons and five daughters. William was still working as a land measurer. One daughter, Sarah Jane, was in service in nearby Coln St Denys but later moved away to work in service in Skipton. By 1891 William Hooper was still working in Sherborne as a land measurer. Three of his sons were then agricultural labourers and five other sons were still at school.

The 1901 census is more explicit on addresses and by then William and Emily were living at no 20 village, Sherborne, probably 2 doors away from the Sherborne Estate Office. William was still a self-employed land measurer and the only children still at home were his son Alick who was a farm worker and his son Bertie. Bertie was born with epilepsy and died at the early age of 25. Ten years later William and Emily were still at the same address, William working as a self-employed land measurer. Their sons Ernest Alick and Frederick George were at home working as labourers. At this time all 11 of their children were still alive. Emily died in 1916 and William Hooper died in 1927, both in the Northleach registration district which included Sherborne. At least six of William Hooper's children moved away from Sherborne variously to Carmarthenshire, Monmouthshire, Coventry, Croyden and Cheltenham.

Another musician who played for the Sherborne Morris, although not on pipe and tabor, was the fiddler **John Mason** who also played for other morris sides – *(see chapter on The Workhouse.)*

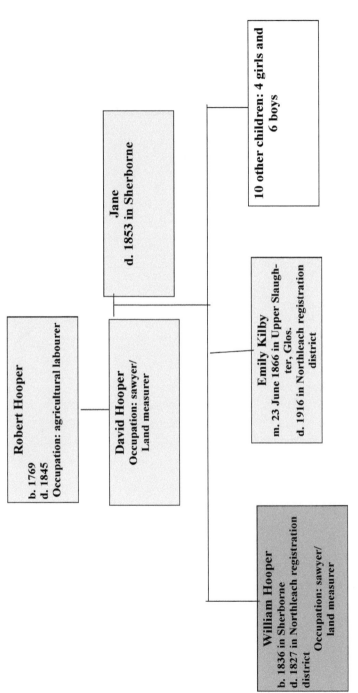

Fig. 12. Family tree for William Hooper

SHERBORNE MUMMERS

The folk of Sherborne, as well as performing songs, tunes and dances, also turned out once a year for the Christmas traditional mummers play, common in many villages of the area. Sherborne was one of over 60 locations in Gloucestershire where mumming was recorded in the 19th and early 20th centuries. These traditional folk plays are usually performed around Christmas time and feature a number of characters dressed in colourful garb. The script is short, comic and spoken in rhyme. The plot usually involves a hero, possibly St George, and a villain, often the Turkish Knight, who fight to the death but are revived by the doctor – but at times it can also be very modern with topical references.

Fig. 13. Gloucestershire Morris mummers

Members of the Pitts and Bunting families were involved in the mummers and the complete play, including its closing song, was collected in around 1930 by the American folk music collector James Madison Carpenter. Carpenter's informant was **William (Mark) Bunting**, brother of Thomas Bunting (*see above*) and William had learnt the closing song from Thomas Pitts (*see above*). The play had characters such as Father Christmas,

Valliant Soldier Bold and the 'Royal and Proosia King' who have a fight and the Doctor to revive them afterwards.

William Bunting was a farm labourer like many of the villagers. He was born in Sherborne and was baptised there on 1 June 1860. He briefly moved to London to work as a stable hand but returned to Sherborne on his marriage to Jane Rouse in Sherborne in 1890 where he continued to work as a labourer. The following year he was working as a gamekeeper like his father in Sherborne, but then in 1901 and 1911 the family were living in his childhood home of Cocklebarrow Cottage in the nearby village of Aldsworth where he was working as an agricultural labourer. He died in 1936 in the same area. According to family trees on www.ancestry.com they had four children, seven grandchildren, eight great-grandchildren and many further descendents.

So although Sherborne was a small village, without even a pub, nevertheless there was a close-knit neighbourhood of singers, dancers and musicians and some of the families intermarried. In such an environment contacts and the passing on of songs and tunes would have been easy given the nearness of houses inhabited by singers and musicians in the village as shown below in some examples. The village is in two parts separated by Sherborne House and Park. It may have been a more compact settlement at one time, but by the 14th century was a large village in two parts distinguished as the West and East Ends. On both sides there are groups of cottages and houses, varying in date from the 17th to the 19th century, but all in a similar style. The east end is bigger than the west, as it was in the 14th century, and less compact. Most of the traditional singers and musicians lived in the west end of the village in Ash Hole Road.

Almost the whole of the east end was rebuilt early in the 19th century as a 'model' village, consisting of groups of cottages, in terraces of 2, 4, and 6, including a row built as

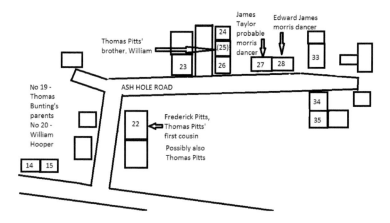

Fig. 14. Plan of part of the west end of Sherborne showing residences of singers and musicians.

almshouses.[6] It was in one of these cottages, number 54, that Thomas Pitts' father, Richard Pitts, lived in later life.

The following tables are taken from the censuses of the relevant years and show the inhabitants of the various cottages in Sherborne in the order in which they appear in the censuses. House numbers only appear in the censuses from 1901 but in some other years it has been possible to extrapolate the houses of tenants. These are shown in brackets. From this can be seen how close the relationships were between the traditional singers and musicians in Sherborne. For example in 1871 it is worth noting that William Bunting, his wife, Emily, and their young children were living next door to Richard Pitts who was the father of another pipe and tabor player, Thomas Pitts. Living on the other side of William Bunting was the Hooper family. Also living 2 doors away from William Hooper was Sarah Pitts and her family. Sarah was the widow of George Pitts, singer and morris dancer Thomas Pitts' grandfather's brother. Thus many of the people making traditional music and singing were close neighbours.

James Hopkins 20 morris musician	William Bunting 25 grandfather of singer Thomas Bunting and mummer William Bunting	Thomas Bunting 40 and Mary Bunting 30, uncle and aunt of singer Thomas Bunting and mummer William Bunting

David Hooper 35, father of morris musician William Hooper also living in this house	Thomas Pitts 70 and Mary Pitts 60, grandparents of singer and morris musician Thomas Pitts

Figs. 15 & 16. Sherborne 1841

Thomas Hooper 60, uncle of morris musician William Hooper	William Bunting 77, and wife Elizabeth Bunting, great-grandparents of morris musician Thomas Bunting	Thomas Pitts 72, grandfather of singer and morris musician Thomas Pitts	Jacob Hooper 32, first cousin of morris musician William Hooper	James Hopkins 31, morris musician with his father Joseph Hopkins

Fig. 17. Sherborne 1851

		(20)	(19)	(22)
Edward James 40 morris dancer	Sarah Pitts 48, widow of morris musician Thomas Pitts' grandfather's brother, George	William Hooper 34, morris musician	William Bunting 10, mummer, with parents James and Mary Bunting	Richard Pitts 47, Father of singer and morris musician Thomas Pitts

Fig. 18. Sherborne 1871

	(20)	(19)		
	William Hooper 40, Morris musician	James Bunting 48 and Mary Bunting 49, Parents of singer Thomas Bunting and mummer William Bunting		

Fig. 19. Sherborne 1881

			(20)		(25)
Frederick Pitts 23 and wife Maria, son of George and Sarah Pitts, Richard Pitts' brother	Thomas Bunting 28, singer, living with his father and grandfather		William Hooper 54 morris musician	(4 houses)	William Pitts 31 and wife Rachel, son of Richard Pitts, brother of Thomas Pitts, singer

Fig. 20. Sherborne 1891

House No.	20	19	22	22	24
Estate Office	William Hooper 64, morris musician and wife Emily 56	James Bunting 68 and daughter Susannah 29, Parents of singer Thomas Bunting and mummer William Bunting	Frederick Pitts 43 and wife Maria 43, son of Sarah Pitts, Widow of morris musician Thomas Pitts' g'father's brother, George	Hills family sharing the house	

Fig. 21. Sherborne 1901

25	26	27	28	29	54
William Pitts 41 and wife Rachel 31 brother of singer and morris musician Thomas Pitts	Emily Hawker 55 widow	James Taylor 50 possible morris dancer	Edward James 70 and wife Emma 61, morris dancer	William Pitts Junior 38, nephew of singer and morris musician Thomas Pitts	Richard Pitts 77 Father of singer and morris musician Thomas Pitts

Fig. 22. Sherborne 1901

House No.	25	26	27	28
	William Pitts 51 and wife Rachel 41 brother of singer and morris musician Thomas Pitts		James Taylor 60 possible morris dancer and wife Anne Taylor 65	Emma James 71 widow of Edward James morris dancer

Fig. 23. Sherborne 1911

54
Richard Pitts 87 Father of singer and morris musician Thomas Pitts living with daughter Sarah and her husband Frederick Drinkwater in their grocer and confectioner's

Fig. 24. Sherborne 1911

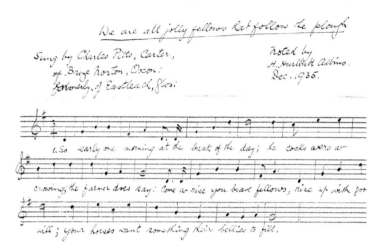

Song from Sherborne sung by Charles, son of Thomas Pitts

Source: Geo. Simpson, sung, Coll. Cecil Sharp, 24 March 1910 at Upton, Didcot, Berks, no 2458

Morris Dance Tune from Sherborne (with instructions for music to be played for various parts of the dance)

Forest of Dean

The Forest of Dean has always had a character of its own with its own dialect and customs and its network of small villages and towns nestling amongst hills and trees. It has an abundance of local flora and fauna, including wild boar. Music making in the area these days is marked with male voice choirs and brass bands but in the past it has had a good variety of traditional songs and music. Although folklorists came too late to recover the once prolific morris dance tradition apart from a quantity of tunes, they did manage to obtain background information on the tradition. It was also the area for traditional carols and a number of these were collected from singers in the Forest of Dean area. From the Forest itself and from its edges came many traditional tunes.

It was also an area frequented by gypsy camps and Cecil Sharp found an important source in **Kathleen Williams** in the Mitcheldean area. Sharp was so struck with her songs that he sought her out in 3 different locations as she moved around. (*See Chapter 4 Gypsy Singers for more information on Kathleen Williams.*)

CINDERFORD

The Forest of Dean was a centre for coal mining. It is believed that iron ore has been mined and smelted in the area of Cinderford since Norman times but in 1800 Cinderford began to flourish as a coal mining area. Collieries such as the Lightmoor, the Northern, the Trafalgar and the Cinderford Bridge collieries were big employers in the area. As elsewhere, the coal mines finally closed in the 1960s.[7] However, only one Forest of Dean mining song has come down to us, namely The Jovial Foresters, a song still found occasionally to this day in the repertoire of local choirs.

However, we do know some of the carols that miners sang. The **Partridge family** from Cinderford had a number of these carols including the rare *Cherry Tree carol* which Maud Karpeles and Pat Shaw collected from John Partridge on 22 August 1952. On 14th July 1994, the collector Roy Palmer visited the family again and collected *The Cock Fled Up in the Yew Tree (a version of I wish you a Merry Christmas), Shepherds of Old* and *With Joy Awake,* from John Partridge's son Stan and and his wife Gwen. Stan was then aged 80 and had been a miner like his father. Stan and Gwen told Roy Palmer that they used to sing carols straight after midnight on Christmas Eve.

The Partridge family has deep roots in the Forest of Dean area and most of the men of the family went into mining. John Partridge's great-grandfather, Richard Partridge was originally from Standish where he was born about 1776. He married Mary Langstone from Newnham in 1802 and by 1841 they were living at Cocklebrook, Standish East, with a probable son, Francis Partridge, where Richard was working as an agricultural labourer. Another of their sons, Joseph, who was John's grandfather, was baptised in Standish in 1819 and became a collier and it was this son who moved to the Forest of Dean. By 1841 Joseph was living at Soudley, with another collier, Edward Robinson and his family. Joseph Partridge married Ann James, a servant, at Newnham in 1846. Their level of literacy appears to have been low as all parties signed this wedding register by mark. By 1851 Joseph and Ann were living in Ruddle, Newnham with three children, Hannah born about 1847 , Mary Ann born about 1849 and Emma born 1851, all born in Newnham, where Joseph was working as a labourer. They had a son, Alfred, John Partridge's father, who was born at The Forge, Soudley and baptised in Newnham on 21 October 1860. By 1861 Joseph and Ann were living near Ruspidge where Joseph was working as a collier. They then had three more children, as well as Alfred, then aged 6. All the children were born in Newnham. Joseph Partridge died in 1866 in the Westbury on Severn registration district which included Newnham. His widow, Ann, continued to live in Lower Ruspidge and in 1871 she was living there with four of her children: Mary Ann who was unmarried, Harriet, Alfred aged 10 and another son, John born about 1864. By 1881 Alfred Partridge, John Partridge's father, was still living near Ruspidge with his mother, then calling herself Ann Bayliss, a widow, and his brother, John aged 16. Both Alfred and John were colliers.

John Partridge's father, Alfred married Elizabeth Hardwick in 1885 and by 1891 they were living in Short Row, Ruspidge with their son, John Partridge then aged 3, and two other children, all born in Ruspidge where Alfred was working as a coal miner. The family continued to live in Ruspidge and by 1911 had six more children, Alfred born about 1897, Dorothy born about 1899 , Harriett born about 1901, Elsie born about 1904, Arthur born about 1906 and Cecil born about 1910. Alfred, John and William were all coal miners: Alfred was a colliery hewer and John and William were colliery labourers underground. Alfred and Elizabeth had 13 children of whom 11 were still alive in 1911. Alfred died in September 1945 in the Forest of Dean registration district.

John William Partridge continued to work as a coal miner and married Mildred Frances Glastonbury of Littledean on 7 March 1915 at Cinderford St John. Their son, William Stanley Partridge, (Stan) was born on the 10 April 1916.

William Stanley Partridge of 176 Ruspidge Road, Cinderford married Gwendolin Vera Sterry, a cook, aged 21 of Huntley Court on 1 August 1938, His father, John William Partridge, was working at the time as a miner colliery fitter. Both parties were able to sign the register and John Partridge signed the register as a witness. John William Partridge aged 75 of 176 Ruspidge Road, Ruspidge, died in 1963 and was buried on 26 August 1963 at Cinderford.

Stan's wife, Gwen was born 16 September 1916 and died in May 2002 aged 85 also in the Forest of Dean registration district. Stan died in 1999 aged 83 in the registration district of the Forest of Dean.

An intriguing source of songs in the Forest of Dean were the **Fletchers**, a gypsy family in the Cinderford area that Cecil Sharp visited in 1919. (*See Chapter 4 Gypsy Singers for more details about this family.*)

BROCKWEIR

Fig. 25.

Brockweir is a small but attractive village located alongside the River Wye within sight of Chepstow on the opposite bank. It used to have a boat building industry and was the highest point up the River Wye which the larger ships could reach and so became the place where the larger vessels loaded and unloaded. Smaller river craft were sometimes hauled up the river by teams of men transferring goods to and from places as far up-river as Hereford. It is reported that vessels up to 90 tonnes could reach this point from the sea. In front of the Quay House there is a screw and shaft (a propelling mechanism) which is reputed to have come from the Belle Marie, which in 1914 became the last boat to sail to Brockweir. Built in Gloucester in 1860, it was Brockweir's 'market boat' and carried local produce to Bristol on a weekly basis between 1898-1912. Before the cast iron road bridge across the Wye was built in 1904/6, only one narrow road led into the village and access was usually achieved by water, with a ferry taking travellers to and from the Welsh bank. Many of the buildings had river connections, acting as warehouses and although today only one public house remains, there were once 16 inns to satisfy the demands of locals, watermen and shipbuilders! Other interesting buildings include the 16th century Manor House (which stands facing the bridge), the 19th century Moravian Chapel (with its Gothic Windows, Art Nouveau glass and a bellcote) and the Old Malt House (which has a fine Tudor-arched stone doorway)

Until the 20th century Brockweir had a vigorous carolling tradition, separate from whatever was being sung in the churches. The primary source for these carols was **Charley Williams** who was visited by several collectors including Russell Wortley (1963) and Andrew Taylor and Bob Patten (1977). Charley sang them a number of carols including a splendid wassail song, learnt from his father and quite different from the Gloucestershire wassail versions collected in the south of the county

Charley said that about the time of WWI, about ten to twenty wassailers would go out on 5 and 6 January, regarded by many as old Christmas Day. They usually took no instruments except when the brothers **Gilbert and Claude Williams** joined them with an accordion. According to Charley other wassailers were his father, his sister, Annie's husband, **Bill Bailey**, and **Albert Dibden**. Apart from the

Wassail Song, collectors recovered about a dozen carols from Charley, including *While Shepherds Watched, The Black Degree, Pilate's Rule, The Holly and the Ivy, Jacob's Well* and *Our Saviour's Love*.

The carolling families all had ties to this maritime industry. The Williams and Dibden families had strong family ties by marriage as can be seen below.

The Williams family had been in the Brockweir area since the early 19th century and Charley's father and grandfather were both born there. Charley Albert Williams was born in July 1909 and baptised 25 July 1909 in Hewelsfield, the son of Albert Adam Williams, a roadman, and Charlotte Williams of The Common, Hewelsfield. He came to Brockweir at age 29 when he married.

Charley's grandfather had ties to the maritime industry. He was Charles Williams, the son of Nathaniel Williams, born 1770 in Brockweir, a mariner who lived at Hudnalls Farm, St Briavels, with his wife, Elizabeth. The location of the farm was described as 'extra parochial, St Briavels'. Another child of Nathaniel, Hannah Williams, born 1806, married Philip Dibden on 16 Jul 1827[8] thus providing a marital link to the Dibden family.

By 1841 Charley's grandfather, Charles Williams, then a mariner aged 30, had married and he and his wife, Ann, aged 25, from St Briavels. were living in Brockweir, near Hewelsfield. By 1851 Charles was a waterman still living in Hewelsfield with Ann and their five children. The rest of the family were born in Hewelsfield. Also living with them was a servant aged 16 and 2 visitors, both watermen. Their son Albert Adam, Charlie's father, was born in 1853 and another sister, Sarah Jane, was baptised privately on 7 November 1855 when Charles was described as a 'halier' (presumably haulier) of Brockweir. By 1861 Charles had taken over the running of the Sloop Inn, Brockweir but by1871, aged 62, he had moved to Woolaston, St Briavels, and was stated to be a farmer born in Woolaston. By 1881 Charles was living on the Common at St Briavels, a farmer of 20 acres aged 72. By 1891, Ann had died and Charles, aged 82, was living with his daughter, Emma Bowen, then a widow, and her family in Brockweir Village, next to the New Inn, run by Alice Dibden. Charles Williams died in early 1897 in the Chepstow registration district and was buried in Hewelsfield. Charles' daughter Elizabeth married into the Dibden family providing another link between these two carolling families.

Charley's father, Albert Adam, was baptised in Hewelsfield on 17 July 1853. In 1861 Albert aged 17 was living in the Sloop Inn, Brockweir. Also living at home were his older brothers: Charles and William who were watermen and Alfred who was a scholar, as was Albert. His sister, Elizabeth Dibden was also there with her son, William They had two boarders: a ship's carpenter and the other was a waterman, born in Whitchurch, Herefordshire who was still boarding also. The children were all born in Hewelsfield.

Albert Adam Williams was married to Charlotte in 1900 in the Chepstow registration district. Between 1900 and 1916 Albert and Charlotte had six daughters and two sons including Charley, born 1909, who were all baptised in Hewelsfield.

Albert is described as a labourer at two of his daughters' baptisms and as a roadman on the other children's baptisms. He had retired from work by the time of his daughter, Alice's marriage in 1941.

Charley's sister, Ruth Naomi, married a baker, Hector Emmanuel George Heaven and his sister, Alice Maud, married a Welsh electrician, George Lewis.

Charley died in 1983 in the Forest of Dean registration district.

ALBERT DIBDEN

*(See references to Hannah Williams above and Albert Adam's sister
Elizabeth for relationship between the Williams and Dibden families.)*

Caroller Albert Dibden was born 1902 and his birth was
registered in the Chepstow Registration district. In 1911, aged
5, he was living in Brockweir with his mother, Alice Ann, who
was described as single, his brother and sister Bella aged 3 and
Alfred aged 4 and his grandmother Elizabeth, a widow. Alice
was a domestic working at home. All were born in Hewelsfield.
Alice's father was John Dibden, born about 1824, who lived
in Hudnalls, Hewelsfield, a mariner who was the master of
a vessel in 1861 and master of a sloop in 1891. In 1881 aged
56 he was the master of the 'Caerleon' moored in the Castle
Precincts in Bristol. Sailing with him were his son, Alexander
aged 16, Charles Dibden aged 33 and Alexander Williams aged
47, possibly a first cousin of Albert Adam Williams.

By 1901, Albert's grandparents John and Elizabeth had
at least seven children: Charles born about 1846 who was a
waterman in 1861, Alice Ann Dibden (Albert's mother) born
about 1853, Charlot born about 1856, Ely/Eli Henry born
about 1859 who became a carpenter, married Belinda and
had a son Albert James in 1889 when living on Brockweir
Common, Hannah born about 1862, Alexander born about
1865 and Sarah Jane born about 1879. Alexander married
another Alice from Bishops Cleeve. John and Elizabeth also
had a granddaughter, Isabella, born about 1879, who had a
son, also named Albert, when she was single in 1902. John
went to sea until he retired to Brockweir. By 1911 Elizabeth
was widowed and living in Brockweir Village with Albert's
mother, Alice Ann Dibden, and Alice's three children, Albert,
Alfred and Bella.

Albert Dibden died in 1967 in the Chepstow registration
district.

GILBERT WILLIAMS

Wassailler Gilbert James Williams was born on 9 February 1910 and baptised in the Moravian Church in Brockweir on 27 March 1910. His family had lived in the St Briavels/Brockweir area for some time. His grandfather John Williams, born about 1852 and his grandmother, Emma, had at least thirteen children between 1870 and 1888, six boys: John, Walter Albert, Wilson, Alfred Alg.., Wilfred and (Herbert) William, who was a cowman in 1911, and seven girls: Geneve, Mabel Emma, Ada Louise, Edith, Elizabeth Kate, Amy and Ada Jane. In 1881 John was a waterman living on St Briavels Common and in 1891 aged 48, he was living 'Under the Hill' outside the parish of St Briavels still working as a waterman. By 1898 and he was an agricultural labourer and continued in this work at least until 1901. At age 68 in 1911 he was a farmer living in Brook Cottage, Brockweir.

Gilbert's father John Gilbert Williams, also known as John Williams Junior, was born in early 1873. On 10 February 1898 when working as a labourer he married Agnes Eliza Hathaway, born 1877 daughter of James and Sarah Hathaway, in the Moravian Church in Brockweir. Agnes' father was a labourer/waterman from Brockweir Common and both families had lived close to each other 'Under the Hill'. The Moravian Church was the only church in Brockweir at the time and had been built in 1833 at a time when a contemporary writer described Brockweir as being *'noted as a city of refuge for persons of desperate and lawless character. The Lord's Day was kept as a day of unhallowed revelling and desecrated by cock-fighting, gambling and quarrelling'*. The peaceful riverbank setting where the Church is now situated was once the site of much of this revelry. In 1831 a Tintern doctor, worried about the spiritual state of the villagers as well as their physical health, wrote about the situation to the

Moravian Minister in Bristol. The Minister came and spoke to the villagers, and received an encouraging response and so the church was built. The family had close connections with this church as John's aunt, Amy Williams, worked as a servant to the Moravian Minister and went with him as cook when he moved on to Northamptonshire as a Church of England Minister. John and Agnes had at least 5 children, all born in St Briavels and baptised in the Moravian Church, Brockweir including Gilbert James who was born on 9 February 1910. By 1901 John was an agricultural labourer living 'Under the Hill' in 'extra parochial Brockweir', St Briavels next door to his father. In 1911 Gilbert aged 1 was living with his parents, John and Agnes, near John's father in Acacia Cottage, Brockweir where John was mentioned in the Census as a 'gardener domestic'. Gilbert's father, John Gilbert Williams possibly died in 1953.

Claude Williams

Charley Williams referred to carollers Gilbert and Claude Williams as brothers, but this may be incorrect. The only Claude Williams of the same generation in the area was one Claude Frederick Alexander Williams born on 25 February 1908 and baptised in the Moravian Church, the son of Francis Henry Williams, a labourer, and May Grace Williams. Claude's father, Francis Henry Williams, was baptised at Hewelsfield on 20 April 1877, son of Alexander and May Williams of Brockweir, a mariner. Claude's grandfather, Alexander, possibly died in Brockweir in 1887. Francis also had a brother, Alfred Edward Williams, who was born in 1863 and baptised in Hewelsfield on 2 August 1863. Claude's mother, May, possibly died in 1961. Claude Williams possibly married Elsie M Gibson in 1930 in the Bristol Registration District.[9]

MUSICIANS

The Forest of Dean has also been home to some important traditional musicians. The village musicians would have played for all village events from church services to Harvest Homes. The first Forest musician that we know of was a fiddler, Joseph Green, who enjoyed his event rather too much and was reported by the Gloucester Journal of 5 January 1778 as *'On Thursday evening a fidler, very much intoxicated with liquor, fell down in the road near Littledean, and was found the next morning frozen to death.'*

The earliest reference to morris dancing and associated musicians in the Forest of Dean is from 1787 in *The Torrington Diaries* which record the tours through England and Wales of the Hon. John Byng (later 5th Viscount Torrington) between the years 1781 and 1794. The collector Cecil Sharp visited the Forest of Dean after being told that there had been morris dancers in Ruardean and in 1910 he met **Charles Baldwin,** also apparently known as Charlie or George, who was living in the almshouses at Newent, one of a family of musicians who had a large repertoire of tunes used for country and morris dancing and had played in various locations in the Forest of Dean. The Baldwin family had lived in the area for some time: Charles, the son of James and Elizabeth Baldwyn, had been christened (also as Baldwyn) at Newent in 1827 and his grandfather, James, had also been christened and lived in Newent. James had also played the fiddle.

Sharp described Charles Baldwin as being 88 in 1910, though he seems to have been christened in 1827 (he was not necessarily christened in his first year of course). Charles married Eliza (*née* Bowr(e)y or Bowrie) and the family frequently moved between Herefordshire and Gloucestershire, pausing at Ross-on-Wye (Herefordshire) and Dymock (Gloucestershire). Their son **Stephen James**

('Stevie') Baldwin (or Baldwyn as his birth certificate has it), was born in Hereford in 1873. After Stephen's birth his parents took the family back to Newent. According to his son Stephen, Charles Baldwin was 98 when he died, thus in about 1920.

Before Stephen was born his father had played the fiddle for the morris dancers at Clifford's Mesne (pronounced 'mean'), just to the west of Newent, until the dancing stopped in about 1870. Sharp said that Baldwin used to play at all the Whitsuntide wakes, local celebrations which took place in all the neighbouring villages, and gave him some interesting tunes, such as the *Morris March* – the processional march of Cliffords Mesne morris, the *Morris Call* – the fiddler would go to the highest place in the village street at 6 o'clock on Monday morning and there solemnly play the *Morris Call* to summon the morris men. The Call proper is the first 12 bars. The succeeding dance music was 'just to excite 'em'. Baldwin also played for Sharp the tune the *'Wild Morris'* – 'Always played 'em off the green'.

Life in the Forest of Dean – which occupies much of that part of Gloucestershire between the River Severn and the Welsh border – was not always the sylvan idyll its name suggests. Coal has been mined here for more than five hundred years by 'freeminers', men born locally and thereby entitled to mine anywhere in the Forest without hindrance. The Forest has also been a source of iron ore for several centuries, and the focal town of Coleford lays claim to being the place where the modern process of making steel was invented in the 19th century. Charcoal has been produced in the Forest of Dean for use in iron smelting since the 5th Century, but its use declined once coke became readily available in the 18th Century.

Charcoal burners, or 'colliers' as they were usually known, would have to bivouac in the woods for days on end, firstly to watch for and repair any cracks which might appear in the turf walls of the 'stack' inside which the wood was burning, and later, once it had cooled, to recover and bag the charcoal, which would then be carted away, on a string of donkeys, to a forge. In the 19th Century charcoal was produced on an industrial basis at factories in the forest. Charles Baldwin himself worked as a charcoal-burner in 'the woods belonging to Squire Onslow' near Newent.

Fig. 26. Stephen Baldwin

Charles Baldwin clearly passed on his love of fiddle playing to his son Stephen. Stephen was the youngest of eight children. His eldest brother, David, was in his early 20s when Stephen was born, and Stephen would have grown up with the youngest of his brothers and sisters. The family lived in Culvert Street in Newent – the southward continuation of the High Street – which was home to several other families of Baldwins and Bowrys, as well as the Wesleyan Methodist Chapel where his mother had been christened in 1835.

Stephen worked as a plate-layer on the Great Western Railway for all of his working life. During the First World War he served in France with the 13th Battalion of the Gloucestershire Regiment, the 'Glosters', and was invalided out after the Battle of the Somme. He was twice married. In 1901 he was living with his first wife Mary neé Brooks, a laundress, born at Mitcheldean and three years his elder, and their two eldest children at Bilson Green, East Dean, near Cinderford. By 1911 the family were living in Townsend, Mitcheldean. He was survived by his second wife, Grace neé James, who died on 25 January 1960. He had four sons: Reg (described as 80 in 1975, but apparently born in 1900); Charles, 73 in 1975; Alec (b.1901); and Ted; and two daughters, Nora and Olive, from his first marriage. Alec, Nora and Ted all played the banjo, and Ted and Charlie also played the fiddle. Charlie also played the mouth organ and was renowned locally as a bones and spoons player.

Stephen Baldwin inherited his father's fiddle, which Charles Baldwin had bought at a music shop in Hereford, and he in turn passed it on to his own son Charles, who played it until he was forced to give up when rheumatism stiffened the first finger of his left hand. Stephen Baldwin himself had acquired another fiddle which in later life hung on the wall by the chimney in his cottage at Upton Bishop and is now in the possession of the Cambridge Morris Men.

So Stephen was at least a third generation of fiddle players and when he was young he learnt to play by watching his father's fingers as he played and imitating them. *"When I'd just left school something came over me and I asked him to show me how to finger it – he showed how to put my fingers on. The first tune I played was Men of Harlech. I learned to put 'em in tune; somehow I stuck to it. It was like a gift. All of it come to me one after the t'other. Eighteen months later I was playing for dances and all sorts of things. You could tell I'd picked it up quick. I suppose it was my old man being a fiddler, look; it come from him – at any rate, I managed to learn it".*

It was while tracking down descendants of Sharp's sources that Russell Wortley of the Cambridge Morris Men – who toured as the *Travelling Morrice* – first met Stephen Baldwin at the village of Upton Bishop, Herefordshire, where he then lived, in April 1947. A couple of months later he

Fig. 27

returned with the Travelling Morris piling into his drawing room. Stephen took his rosin-covered fiddle down from its hook near the mantelpiece and played a number of tunes.

He was then recorded several times by the song collectors Russell Wortley and Peter Kennedy in the early 1950s. Peter Kennedy recorded several of Stephen Baldwin's tunes in the schoolroom at Upton Bishop on 13 October 1952. One of these was broadcast on Peter Kennedy's radio programme *As I Roved Out*, which was devoted to field recordings of traditional music, and this made a local celebrity of Stephen Baldwin. He had a very large repertoire and it was also quite varied, comprising hornpipes, jigs, marches, country-dances and tunes for morris dances, as well as some song tunes (the majority of the latter surviving only as names on the list provided by his widow). The 'morris dance tunes' are not specific to that purpose (they include *Brighton Camp, Haste to the Wedding*, etc), but they are generally speaking well known folk tunes.

Stephen's son Charlie would also accompany his father in pubs vamping on the piano, and remembered one such occasion at the Crown in Aston Crews (Herefordshire) when his father suddenly stopped playing and said: "Listen! There's a wireless; we're off!" Off they went down the road to the White Hart, where there happened to be a coachload of people from Wales. Stephen and his son Charlie got in by the back door, collected their pints and 'soon got going'.

Stephen's second wife, Grace, also played the piano, and would accompany him when he played the fiddle in the evenings – to discourage him from playing in the pub, it is said, though perhaps maliciously, as many a traditional fiddler also enjoyed playing at home if there was a pianist in the family to play along with.

Stephen Baldwin's friend Bill Williams, the grandson of Jack 'Fiddler' Williams, recounted to Peter Kennedy how he and Stevie Baldwin would go to the clubroom upstairs at the *Yew Tree* on "the Mitcheldean road" and elsewhere where Steven would play. *"The fiddler, he'd sit down in his chair and he'd play the fiddle, you know, and everybody would be having their drink and listening for a time, and then soon as he started on the dancing, see … up they was and holding one another, and round and round and dancing about there in the club room. Well, I've knowed 'em up there as you couldn't hardly get inside the club room at the Cross, where there were so many people go in there … of a night. But I can't remember the names on 'em (the dances) now, but of course, I used to enjoy myself all right with 'em".*

The pre-eminence of the hornpipe in Stephen Baldwin's repertoire, for both the fiddler and his audience, which could be used for solo step dancing, is illustrated by the description which he gave to the local collector and antiquarian H H (Harry Hurlbutt) Albino, of a Gypsy wedding he was invited to provide the music for. Arriving at 3 o'clock in the afternoon, he stayed until 2 o'clock in the morning, perched on a tree stump and playing, in his own words, "nothing but hornpipes", to which the Gypsies danced "with great vigour". "The sweat simply rolled off them. They never seemed to get tired".

Fig 28

Stephen's son Charlie has suggested that his father wanted to involve him in the recording sessions but could never contact him in time because he could not write (apparently Stephen's children and his second wife did not always see eye to eye). Given Stephen Baldwin's apparent preference for a piano accompaniment we can only wonder at our loss.

As well as playing the fiddle and singing popular songs – he was also recorded by Russell Wortley singing a music hall song *Anyone Does For Me* (music by Lilian Bishop, written and performed by Dan Crawley (1872-1912)). Stephen Baldwin was also involved in a local carol singing party.

Stephen Baldwin died at home in Upton Bishop on 24 November 1955, having been afflicted with heart problems for some while. Grace Baldwin had nursed him night and day without medical assistance of any kind, and the last thing he said was 'Mother' as he died in her arms after his last attack. He was buried at Newent as he had wished, with his medals and a Union Jack (lent by Commander Pope RN of Much Marsh) on his coffin.[10]

RUARDEAN

The *Morris Call* tune was also recalled by musician **Henry Allen**, who was living in Stratford Upon Avon aged 90 in 1909 when he told Sharp that he had played for the morris dancers at Ruardean (on the northern edge of the present Forest) "down to about 1871-2" . In subsequent visits to the Forest of Dean Sharp learned that during the week of the Whitsuntide Wakes the Ruardean and other morris sides would go from place to place. There were six dancers in the set. As they marched the Foreman (or "Flagman" as he was called) carried a large white flag three or four feet square embroidered with his initials and the name of the village or trimmed with rosettes; this, on a pole four or five feet long, he waved in time with the music. Alongside him, no.2 of the set carried a sword in each hand which he whirled round his head. The other four dancers followed behind in pairs and they had a fool (with a tail on the end of a stick three or four feet long), a Ragman and a Fiddler. The Swordsman used to dance over the swords on the ground to the tune of Greensleeves.[11]

So overall in the Forest of Dean we see a wealth of traditional singers and musicians singing in different contexts. Unique carols were also popular, as sung by Stan and Gwen Partridge and Mrs Fletcher in Cinderford. Singers in Brockweir went around wassailing and had a fount of local carols which they sang at Christmas. In Mitcheldean gypsy Kathleen Williams had a good stock of songs. From the edges of the Forest of Dean came many traditional tunes, such as those played by Stephen and Charles Baldwin in Newent and various Forest locations.

Wassail Song Brockweir

1. A whistle, a wassail about our town
   The cup it is black and the ale is brown
   The cup it is made of the mulberry tree
   So here, good fellow, we'll drink to thee.

2. Here's to the quick and to the right horn
   Pray God send the master a good crop of corn
   Both wheat, rye and barley and all sorts of grain
   So here, good fellow, we'll drink to thee again.

3. If your missues and master they be not at home
   Or if they be abroad, God send them safe home
   Or if they be at home let them live at ease
   So fetch out the white loaf and the whole cheese.

4. Come all you pretty maidens that reel on your pin
   Pray open the door and let the wassailers in
   For if you are maidens or if you are none
   Pray don't let the wassailers stay on the cold stones. (repeat last two lines)

Source: Sung by Charley Williams (55). Brockweir, in 1964. Recording made in 1964, possibly by Singer Song has also been collected from Charley Williams by Russell Wortley and later Bob Pattern & Andrew Taylor

Notes: Song sung in Brockweir and St Briavels. 'Waissailers' is sung as 'wass-lers'

2

OCCUPATIONS

Trades and occupations have changed drastically over the last hundred and fifty years, from agriculture to factories to offices. Today the wholesale and retail trade is the largest employer of the 16 to 74 age group with 16 per cent (4.2 million) of employed usual residents working in this sector. (2011 Census, Office for National Statistics). However the occupations of our singers at the beginning of the 20th Century were quite different and it is clear that at that time life in Gloucestershire had not changed much since the 17th century. The table on page 46 shows the distribution of Occupational Categories in Gloucestershire 1660-1699 and would be typical of life throughout England for centuries before that[12] *(Fig 29)*.

The limited number of other non-agricultural occupations underlines both the simplicity of rural life and the self-sufficiency of the villagers. Bakers, fishermen, innkeepers, tailors, shoemakers, masons and carpenters served householders' needs.[13] Notably two thirds of the population of villages were employed in agriculture.

Indeed even at the end of the 19th century things had not changed very much according to Bartholemew's Gazetter's words in 1887:

Occupational category	Gloucester	Market towns	Villages	Total
Agriculture	7	67	407	481
Textiles	4	60	76	140
Food and drink	37	24	20	81
Building and allied trades	7	10	25	42
Professions	16	4	18	38
Metalwork	11	6	13	30
Distribution	14	9	2	25
Transport	2	1	16	19
Leatherwork	5	4	6	15
Clothing and footwear	16	14	20	5
Miscellaneous	1	1	2	4
Total	**120**	**200**	**605**	**925**

Fig. 29. Occupational categories in Gloucestershire 1600–1699

'Agriculture forms the leading occupation of the rural population; in the hills sheep-farming receives attention; while the rich valley of the Severn has long been famed for the superiority of its products. Its luxuriant pastures especially have originated and supported a great industry in the shape of dairy farms which produce the celebrated Glo'ster cheese. In the west of the county are 2 great coal fields – the Forest of Dean on the north, and the Bristol coalfield on the west. Other minerals are gypsum, barytes, quartz, limestone, and freestone. The manufactures are mostly woollen and cotton stuffs, but at Bristol there are also large hardware manufactures."[14]

If we then compare this list of trades with those of the performers as listed in www.glostrad.com[15] totalling 239 singers and musicians, we find that the distribution of the occupations of those from whom songs were collected in the earliest part of the 20th century is remarkably similar to that above. Gloucestershire has had a large rural economy and collectors visited many in rural areas who might be expected to retain memories of songs from their youth:

Farmers and other farm staff

6 Farmers and 1 wife of farmer (one farmer is also a beer house keeper, one then becomes a council worker, 1 farmer is also a writer)

1 farm bailiff

27 agricultural labourers

12 carters and 1 wife of carter

1 engine driver on farm

Animal Husbandry

15 shepherds and 2 wives of shepherds

(2 of the carters were also cattlemen)

2 grooms and 2 wives of grooms (1 groom is also a cattleman)

1 horseman on farm

Other Country Occupations

4 blacksmiths

4 woodmen

1 gamekeeper and 1 wife of a gamekeeper

    (1 agricultural labourer is also a gamekeeper)

    (1 sack contractor is also a gamekeeper)

Servants

3 cooks

2 housemaids

1 lady's maid

1 parlourmaid

1 footman

Stone and Quarry workers
2 stone masons and 1 daughter of a stone quarryman
3 agricultural labourers and 1 labourer are also quarrymen
1 jobbing mason

As time went on newer employment opportunities came in such as in road building and industrial works.

Building Trade
1 building works manager
1 daughter of builder
1 builder's labourer
    (1carter is also a builder)
4 carpenters
1 plasterer
1 tiler

Businessmen and businesswomen
1 businessman
1 merchant
1 boarding house keeper
1 baker
1 cider maker
1 grocer
1 printer and 1 wife of printer
1 wood dealer and 1 wife of wood dealer
1 coal dealer (one of the travellers was also a coal dealer)
1 sack contractor
1 clockmaker
1 shoemaker
    (1 traveller is also a shopkeeper)
    (1 farmer is also a beer house keeper)
Other crafts
1 cordwainer

1 electrician
1 engineer
2 glovers
1 machine setter
1 musician
1 basketmaker

Railway workers
1 foreman railway platelayer
1 railway platelayer
1 railway labourer

Other employment
2 miners
1 clothworker
1 rag sorter and mill hand
1 charwoman then midwife
1 laundress
1 driver
2 postmen
3 roadmen and 1 road labourer
1 sand and gravel worker
1 sailor
1 sexton

The above show the trades and occupations of the traditional Gloucestershire singers listed on the website. Let us now look in more detail at the lives of some of these performers.

AGRICULTURAL LABOURERS

These formed approximately two thirds of the population and the skills involved would be passed on from generation to generation and many people remained in the area of their birth throughout their lives. A typical agricultural labourer would be **Henry Corbett** of Snowshill.

Henry Corbett sang *The Irish Girl, The Cuckoo, Lord Bateman* and *Toby* on 9 April 1909 to Cecil Sharp and then on a second visit on 13 August 1909 he sang him *The Derby Ram, King George, The Shannon Side* and *Shepherds Are The Best Of Men.*

Henry's father was James Corbett, then spelled Corbit, an agricultural labourer, born in Snowshill about 1813. In 1841 James and Anne Corbett née Chandler from Stanway were living in Snowshill with their children William and Sarah, both baptised in Snowshill: William on 8 January 1837 and Sarah on 19 May 1839 although the records show that James and Ann did not marry until 1843 in the Winchcombe registration district when Ann was about 32 years old. Their son Henry was born in Snowhill in 1849.

Living next door to them was another agricultural labourer, William Corbit (Corbett) aged 55 born in Guiting Power, presumably a relation. William had other children, Sally aged 20, William aged 16 and James aged 10 and possibly a grandson John aged 4 months.

In 1851 the family was still living in Snowshill – Henry and 3 of his siblings were living at home, namely William, an agricultural labourer aged 14, Charles baptised 29 January 1843 and his sister, Sarah aged 11.

William Corbett was still living next door with his unmarried daughter, Sally, son William and his wife Fann(a)y and their daughter, Ann who was 8 years old.

1861 found the family still in Snowshill where James was

working as an agricultural labourer. The only two children still at home were Henry, then aged 10, and his brother, William, also an agricultural labourer. All the family were then said in the 1861 Census to have been born in Snowshill.

By 1871 Henry's siblings had all moved out and Henry aged 22 was the only child still living at home with his parents in Snowshill Street, Snowshill.

William Corbett and his wife Fanny (see above) were also still in Snowshill Street with a daughter, Hannah aged 10 and a lodger.

Henry Corbett married Mary Ann Tombs sometime between April and June 1876 in Winchcombe registration district. By 1881 aged 31 he was living in a cottage in Snowshill Village next to the village shop with his wife Mary Ann, then aged 32, born in Stow in the Wold. He was working as an agricultural labourer. His parents were also still living in Snowshill. His father was still working as an agricultural labourer at the time of the census. Also living with James was James' grandson, Henry Corbett a ploughboy aged 12 born in Snowshill, the son of Henry's brother, Charles. But shortly afterwards Henry's father, James Corbett, died aged 72 and was buried at Snowshill on 29 March 1881. His wife, Ann died and was buried in Snowshill on 26 January 1885.

In 1891 Henry and Mary Ann, aged 42 and 43 respectively, were still living in Snowshill Village where Henry was working as a labourer. In 1901 they were still in Snowshill with Henry aged 51 working as a farm labourer as he was again in 1911 at age 62. They never had any children.

William Corbett's wife, Fanny, had died but he was still living in Snowshill, aged 69 until he died in 1900.

Henry Corbett died in December 1925 in Winchcombe registration district. His nearest living descendents would be from the families of his brothers and sister.

Many agricultural labourers had large families because of

poor income and sometimes young children started work very early as ploughboys. Agricultural labourers also sometimes found work as shepherds. One such person was **John Hawker** of Broad Campden who was probably the Mr Hawker who sang the tale of *William Taylor* to Percy Grainger and Eliza Wedgwood on 4 April 1908, the story of a jilted girl who takes revenge on her lover by dressing as a soldier, tracking him down and shooting him. In the song, her commanding officer is so impressed with this action that he immediately promotes her. It seems unlikely that attempted murder would meet with the same approval these days.

John Hawker was born in Grafton, Beckford about 1834. By 1851 he had left home and was working as a farm labourer and living in the house of John Nind, a farmer of 100 acres employing four labourers in Dumbleton. He married Ann Spiers in the Winchcombe registration district at the end of 1857. Ann had been born in Ashton Under Hill. In 1861 they were living in Beckford with two children, Mary Ann born about 1858 and Charles born about 1860, both born in Dumbleton. John and Ann moved around with his work over the years. By 1871 John and Ann were living in Grafton near Pershore with four more sons, William born about 1863, Hubert born about 1865, Arthur born about 1867 and Martin born about 1868, all born in Grafton. John and Ann were both working as farm labourers. By 1881 they had moved to Badsey where John was working as a shepherd and his son, Arthur, as a ploughboy. They had another three sons, Edwin born about 1871, Joseph born about 1875, both born in Grafton, and Frank born about 1877 in Saintbury and two daughters, Faith Ada born 1879 and Laura, born about 1881 in Cow Honeybourne. By 1891 they had moved to Lapstone Cottage, Broad Campden where John continued working as a shepherd and his son, Frank, as a ploughboy. By 1901 John and Ann were living in Broad Campden where John continued to work as an agricultural labourer. The only child still at home was Laura Hawker. By 1911 as old age pensioners they had moved back to Grafton. By then they had 11 children all still living. John Hawker probably died in the Kidderminster registration district in Worcestershire in 1922.

The previous year, Grainger and his collaborator Eliza Wedgwood had visited one **Mrs Mary Hawker** in Broad Campden, noting several songs. There is no married couple John and Mary Hawker in the censuses and, given that Mr Hawker's wife was Ann, not Mary, we are talking of someone else, possibly John's [unmarried] sister Mary, although Grainger's mention of **Mrs** Hawker confuses the issue. Their 1908 visit was a return trip to see Mary, when John contributed the one song *William Taylor*.

QUARRYMEN

Cotswold limestone has always been favoured for building – it was the local stone in Gloucestershire and its golden colour lends character to the local cottages. Many people were employed in the local quarrying industry and amongst them we find more of our singers.

Children very often inherited their parents singing ability and songs were passed down through families. One such family was that of **William Newman,** a labourer and stone quarryman from Stanton.

On 17 November 1907, Percy Grainger, staying in Stanton at Eliza Wedgwood's house, collected songs from William Newman, namely *The Farmer's Boy, The Saucy Sailor* and *Where You Going To, My Pretty Maid*. This was probably the William George Newman described below. The following day Grainger noted in a letter to Karen Holten, his Danish girlfriend, '*Mother and I stayed with a dear old maid, Miss (Eliza)*

Wedgwood (at The Bank, Stanton) …in the afternoon 4 men came there to her house and 2 of them were good; and give me hope about the district.' The other 'good' singer was John Collett.

Quite a lot is known of William Newman and his family. His father, also called William, married Kezia Dyer in the second quarter of 1869 in the Winchcombe registration district which included Stanway. Their son William George was baptised on 6 June 1869 in Stanway. By 1871 they were living with Kezia's parents, John and Mary Dyer, in Stanway where William and John were both working as labourers, with two children, William George and Ann born about 1871. By 1881 William and Kezia were living in a cottage in Stanway where William senior was working as an assistant gardener. Kezia's father was a widower living with them and described as previously employed in forests. William and Kezia had more children, John born about 1872, Raymond born about 1877 and Mary born about 1880. A further daughter, Flora, followed in about 1884 and shortly after that William senior died. Kezia remarried to William Stratford, a labourer of Church Stanway in 1889 in Stanway. In 1891 Kezia and William Stratford were living in a cottage in Stanway where William was working as a general labourer. Kezia's children, including William George, were living with them and they had a daughter of their own, Minnie Stratford, born in 1891. Census returns show that William worked as a labourer and assistant gardener

Grainger's informant William George married Ellen Childs from Upper Sapey in Herefordshire, the daughter of a roadman, on 8 January 1895. In 1901 they were living in Stanway with three children, Ellen A. Newman born about 1897, Florence Audrey Newman born about 1898 and William Arthur Newman born about 1900 when William George was working as a cattleman on a farm. They also had a lodger who was a gamekeeper. In 1911 they were still living in Church Stanway. Florence had left home. William was by then working as a stone quarryman and they had a different lodger. He died and was buried in Stanway on 10 December 1941.

Sometime between 1927 and 1935 William Newman sang *The Outlandish Knight* to the American folklorist James Madison Carpenter at Stanway. Although Carpenter noted all the words to William's old ballad of the Outlandish Knight, he did not write out the tune, only saying that he had learnt the song 50 years previously and that tune was the "same as Nightingale", obviously referring to Arthur Nightingale, another of Carpenter's singers, who lived in nearby Didbrook. Unfortunately, Nightingale's tune has not been preserved either.

William George Newman's daughter, Florence Audrey Newman, married Donald Munro Grant, a police constable from Ayr, on 12 August 1921 when her stepsister, Minnie Kezia Stratford, was a witness and her father was described as a forester.

Another singing Newman, Albert Newman who was visited on 30 November 1957 by the collector Brian Ballinger. Albert, who was in his 50s was living in Tiltup Cottage, Southrop, and was in his 50s who said that he remembered his father being collected by Alfred Williams.

SHEPHERDS

Grazing sheep brought in much money to the Cotswolds which were famous for their Cotswold Lion sheep and even in the thirteenth century many people were working in the wool industry. Cotswold wool was very popular and fleeces were very prized in Britain and overseas. More recently many were employed either as shepherds looking after the sheep or in the mills manufacturing woollen cloth. This resulted in many singers favouring songs about their employment as shepherds who were a fruitful source of traditional songs. No doubt they had plenty of time to amuse themselves out on the Cotswolds and on their return to the village. We know of the following singing shepherds in Gloucestershire, but in all likelihood most Gloucestershire shepherds would have been able to sing a song:

Name of shepherd	Location	Date and name of song collector
Ash, George	Ampney Crucis	Between 1913 and 1916 Alfred Williams
Avery, John	Aldsworth	Between 1913 and 1916 Alfred Williams
Barrett, Shepherd	Lechlade	Between 1913 and 1916 Alfred Williams
Carpenter, Robert	Cerney Wick	Between 1913 and 1916 Alfred Williams
Clappen, Thomas	Driffield	Between 1927 and 1935 James Madison Carpenter
Coldicote, Thomas	Ebrington	Published 19th century
Evans, Joseph	Old Sodbury	3 April 1907 Cecil Sharp
Hawker, Mr.	Broad Campden	4 April 1908 Cecil Sharp
Hedges, William	Chipping Camden	1909 (11 Aug, 14 Aug, 16 Aug, 28 Aug and 10 Sep) Cecil Sharp
Phelps, Charles	Avening	Between 1927 and 1935 James Madison Carpenter

GEORGE ASH

One such singing shepherd was **George Ash** who sang *Here's Away to the Downs* to Alfred Williams sometime between 1913 and 1916 in Ampney Crucis. The song was originally *"Hark,*

Hark away to the Downs", a rather precious hunting song which was printed in the late 18th century. George's version appears to be the only version collected in oral tradition.

Several villages with 'Ampney' in their name are situated to the east of Cirencester along the brook of that name, the largest being Ampney Crucis. Ampney St Mary is much smaller and fell into disuse from the 18th century onwards and was amalgamated in many aspects with nearby Ampney St Peter. George Ash's family lived in all three of these villages. The curate in Ampney St Peter made some notes on life in the village in 1811 and 1821 when most of the families were employed in 'husbandry and labour' and the supporting 'trade or handicraft'.

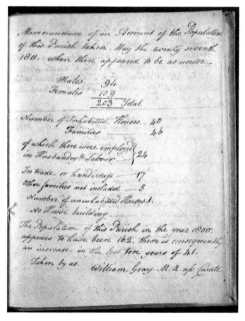

Fig. 30.

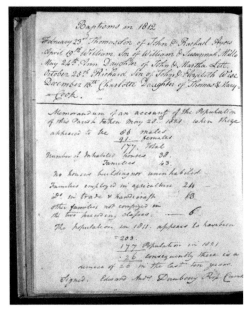

Fig. 31.

George Ash was born in Ampney St Mary, otherwise
known as Ashbrook, and baptised there on 16 February 1845,
the son of Joseph and Ellen Ash. Two previous generations of
his family lived in the Ampneys. His grandfather, Edward Ash,
was a labourer and on 15 November 1795 he and his wife,
Mary baptised their daughter, Susannah, in Ampney St Peter
Church. George's father, Joseph Ash, was born in Ampney St
Mary about 1811 and on 15 June 1831 was living in Ampney
St Peter where he married Ellen Evans also from Ampney St
Peter. Joseph and Ellen had at least ten children, James born
about 1834, Elizabeth born about 1837, Sarah born about
1838, John, baptised on 26 October 1839 and five more, born
in Ampney St Mary, to where the family had moved by then
and Joseph was working as a labourer, namely: Edwin born
about 1841, Mary born about 1843, George born in 1845,
Harriet born about 1848 and Joseph born about 1849 and Lucy

Ann born about 1859. Joseph continued to live in a cottage in Ampney St Mary, working as an agricultural labourer, and the couple had another daughter. By 1861 George, his sister, Harriet and brother, Joseph, were all working as agricultural labourers at the young ages of 16, 14 and 12 respectively.

In 1867 George married Jane Spring Tilling from Ampney St Mary and by 1871 was working as a shepherd and living in a cottage in Ampney Crucis with Jane and their two children, George baptised 13 September 1868 in Ampney St Mary and Emily Jane baptised in Ampney Crucis on 15 April 1871. The family continued to live in Ampney Crucis where George continued to work as a shepherd and by 1881 they had four further children all born in Ampney Crucis: Arthur James born 1872, Margaret Ellen baptised on 24 May 1874, Alice Mary baptised 2 April 1876 in Ampney St Mary, and John baptised 28 December 1879. By then his son George was working as a ploughboy.

George's mother, Ellen, had died at the end of 1869 aged 58 but on 17 January 1874 his father remarried to Harriet Page from Barnsley who was three years younger than him and had not previously been married. They lived at Hilcot End, Ampney Crucis. By 1881 George and his father were living next door to each other in Ampney St Mary.

George and Jane Ash then had a daughter, Elsie Jane, who was baptised in Ampney Crucis on 17 October 1886 followed by a son Charles who was baptised in Ampney Crucis on 23 July1892. George continued to work as a shepherd and by 1891 the only child still living at home in Dudley Cottage, Ampney Crucis was Margaret who was working as a general servant at home. Dudley Cottages numbers one, two and three still exist there. That same year George's father, Joseph, died and was buried in Ampney St Mary. His second wife, Harriet, died in 1896 and was buried in Ampney Crucis. George Ash's wife, Jane, died in Ampney Crucis and was buried there on 15 June

1898. George continued to work as a shepherd living 'near cemetery' in Ampney Crucis, with his daughters, Margaret and Jennie, and his son, Charles, who was working as an agricultural labourer, according to the 1901 census. He was still there working as a shepherd in 1911 living with his unmarried daughter, Margaret, his son, Charles, who was still working as an agricultural labourer and his daughter, Jane who had married a Mr Talbot two years previously and had one son, Harold, aged one born in Coxwell, Berkshire. By then George had been married for 30 years and had 9 children all still living.

George Ash died in 1924 in the Cirencester registration district. His daughter Margaret died unmarried in June 1947 in the Cirencester registration district. George's son John married Rosetta Winifred Haines of 60 Gloucester Street, Cirencester, the daughter of a labourer on 26 December 1904 in Cirencester and by 1911 they were living in Harnhill, Cirencester where John was working as a cowman with two daughters, Margaret born abut 1906 and Winifred born 1910.

JOHN AVERY

John Avery was born in Langford, Berkshire on the eastern side of the Cotswolds on the Gloucestershire/Berkshire/Oxfordshire border, in about 1810, the son of Elijah Avery, a labourer. Working as a shepherd he came to live with farmer Richard Waine, at Aldsworth, who had a large farm of 419 acres with 12 labourers. The following year on 11 October 1852 he married Anne Peacey, the daughter of a labourer who was about 12 years younger than him. John had had some education as he was able to sign his name. Their son, **William Avery**, was baptised in Aldsworth on 31 July 1853 and by 1871 he had left home and was working in Bibury as an under carter and lodging in the household of one Thomas Tea. John Avery continued to work as a shepherd, living at Green Farm, Aldsworth and died in the Northleach registration district, which included Aldsworth, in 1879. By 1881 his son William had moved back in with his mother, Ann, then aged 59, when William was working as an agricultural labourer. That same year William Avery married Caroline Hicks, the daughter of singer George Hicks, and by 1891 they were living in Aldsworth village with 4 sons, John M. born about 1892, Edward P. Born about 1893, Joseph born about 1885 and a daughter, Sarah A(nnie), born about 1888. By 1901 William was still working as an agricultural labourer. His son, Joseph, was still living at home working as a carter on a farm, as was his daughter, Sarah A(nnie). He also had another son, Elijah, born about 1894. Joseph and Elijah were still living at home in 1911 with William and Caroline as William continued his work as an agricultural labourer. His daughter, Sarah Annie, married Arthur Akers from Eastnor who worked in farming from Ladbarrow Cottages in Aldsworth and had at least two children there.

The song collector Alfred Williams collected two songs from William Avery between 1913 and 1916, *Leather Breeches* and *The Ploughman*. About *Leather Breeches* he stated *'This old song was popular in Gloucestershire between Tetbury and Burford. I have not heard it south of the Thames though no doubt it was sung there formerly.'* He also said that *'This was sung for many years by George Hicks of Aldsworth, formerly of Sherborne, an old Morris dancer.'* The links between the Avery and Hicks family continued to be very close as also living with the family in 1911 was Caroline's mother, Emma Hicks, a laundress aged 66 who was the widow of singer George Hicks of Aldsworth, formerly of Sherborne. Alfred Williams also said that the song *The Ploughman* was 'as sung by John Avery, Aldsworth', William's father, so William sang Alfred Williams these two songs which he had learned from his father and his father-in-law. William Avery died in 1930.

THOMAS COLDICOTT

One song which was popular with shepherds as well as other rural singers was *We Shepherds Are the Best of Men* which was sung, among others, by **Thomas Coldicott** – information on him was given to Lucy Broadwood and J. A. Fuller Maitland by F. Scarlett Potter of Halford, Shipston on Stour. This song, under the name of *The Shepherd Song,* was published in English County Songs in 1893 where it was stated that the first verse was taken from the recitation of a lady born at Stoke, Gloucestershire in 1793 and the remaining verses were recovered from Thomas Coldicott, shepherd of Ebrington, Gloucestershire, known in dialect as Yubberton and the butt of several jokes about the simpletons of Yubberton. According to the folklorist Steve Gardham, the Shepherd song is an adaptation of an earlier sailor ballad printed on broadsides 'When the stormy winds do blow'. In Gloucestershire it was also sung by a groom from Lechlade, John Puffet, who also lived in Southrop, and by Peter Gill, an agricultural labourer from Sheepscombe and doubtless by countless others.

Although Thomas Coldicott was stated to be a shepherd as described above, census returns show him to have been an agricultural labourer. Thomas was born in Ebrington in 1838, the son of William Coldicott, a blacksmith and his wife, Sarah, formerly Phillips. In 1841 William and Sarah were living in Ebrington with Thomas and their other children, William born about 1827, Mary born about 1830, John born about 1833 and Emma born about 1835. Shortly afterwards in 1842 Thomas' father, William, died and in 1848 his mother, Sarah, remarried to John Boseley, a labourer and widower also from Ebrington. By 1851 Thomas was living with them in Ebrington with John's son, also called John.

By 1861 Thomas had left home and was living at Samuel Goff's Pasture Farm, Alveston, Warwickshire, working as a groom. Goff was a farmer of 350 acres employing 8 men and 5 boys. In 1864 Thomas married Ann Butler, who was born in Chipping Campden, in the Shipston on Stour registration district which included Ebrington and in 1871 they were living in Ebrington Street where Thomas was working as a labourer. They had many children, Emma baptised 30 July 1865, Kate baptised 12 August 1866, Rosa J. born 1868 and William born 1870, all born in Ebrington and by 1881 they were living at 55 Ebrington and had a further four children, John Henry born about 1874, Mary Ann born about 1876, Georgiana born about 1878 and Mercie born 1880. By this time, Thomas and Ann and their son, William, were all working as agricultural labourers and their daughter, Rosa, was an unemployed domestic servant. Thomas and Ann continued to live at 55 Ebrington and in 1891 Thomas was still living there and working as an agricultural labourer. The only children still living at home were John and Mercie. Thomas Coldicott died in 1892 in the Shipston on Stour registration district.

Thomas' Children

According to a family tree on www.ancestry.com, **Thomas' daughter, Kate Coldicott**, married John Simmonds in Tipton, Staffordshire on 20 October 1894. They settled in Walsall, Staffordshire, and had at least four children, Sidney J. Simmonds born 1896 and died 1936, Albert James Simmonds born 1893 and died in 1989, Margaret May Simmonds who was born and died in 1925 and Joyce Simmonds born 1932 and died in 2002. Sidney Simmonds married Hilda J.Mills and died in 1936. Thomas' daughter, Kate Simmonds, died in Walsall, Staffordshire in 1898.

Thomas' son, John Henry Coldicott, married Caroline Charlotte Currus in 1894 in the Shipston on Stour registration district. They had at least two sons, Maurice William Coldicott born 1895 and William Arthur Stanley Coldicott born 1900. They emigrated to St John, New Brunswick on 15 April 1910. Their son, Maurice William, died in Vancouver on 31 January 1970.

Thomas' daughter, Rosa Coldicott married John Henry Flint, a groom, who was born about 1864 in Blackwell, Worcestershire. By 1911 they were living in Wayfield Cottage, Snitterfield, Warwickshire. They had been married for 21 years and had seven children all still living with them, Robert John born about 1891, George Frederick born about 1894, Thomas Edward born about 1901, Mary Jane born about 1903 – all born in Ilmington – and Kate Elizabeth born about 1886, Elsie May born about 1897 and Lucy Emma born about 1910. The last three children were all born in Todenham, just over the border in Gloucestershire.

WILLIAM HEDGES

Fig. 32. Museum of English Rural Life, University of Reading

The shepherd William Hedges was a prolific source of songs for the collector Cecil Sharp who visited him on five occasions in August and September 1909. He sang 15 songs, all representative of a country singer's repertoire, mainly songs about courting and life in the countryside but also some other favourites such as *The Golden Vanity* about a young cabin boy who was a hero deceived by his captain. He was also another Gloucestershire shepherd who actually sang the song *We Shepherds Are The Best Of Men*. On 10 August 1909, Sharp noted "knows no shepherd songs" – he had become aware of the song *We Shepherds are the Best of Men* which seemed popular amongst the county's shepherd singers and hoped to find it here. A couple of weeks later, on his third meeting with William, he did manage to get him to sing him this song. Other songs which William Hedges sang were *The Broken-hearted Gentleman,* courting songs *The Crafty Maid's Policy, Fifty Long Miles, Horses to Grass, I Followed her* and *Pretty Nancy of Yarmouth,* cautionary tale *Taffy,* and the Gloucestershire song *John Ridler's Oven.* [16]

William Hedges' family had been living in Hannington in Wiltshire, just over the border from Gloucestershire, going back to his great-grandfather, Henry Hedges, who was born there in 1754, his grandfather, William, born there in 1774 and his father, Henry, who was baptised there on 18 February 1803. Henry, an agricultural labourer, married Martha Pipkin from nearby Inglesham on 11 October 1830 and William was baptised in her home village of Inglesham on 23 February 1831. By 1841 the family were living at Curtiss Farm, Hannington, where William's father, Henry, was working as an agricultural labourer. At that time William had three younger brothers, Joseph, Charles and Isaac. In 1851 the family were still living in Hannington where William aged 18 was working as an agricultural labourer like his father. He also had another younger brother, Henry.

On 23 September 1854 William Hedges married Emma

Wright from Alcester, Worcestershire, at St Thomas' Church, Birmingham. He was still working as a labourer. They went to live in Oversley Green near Alcester, Worcestershire, and had two daughters who were baptised in Arrow, Worcestershire: Hannah in 1857 and Fanny Ann in 1859. About 1860 the family moved to Cleeve Prior where William was working as a shepherd and they had a son, William Henry, that year. In 1863 they had another son, Thomas, but by the time of the birth of their next son Charles in 1865, the family had moved to Gloucestershire and were living in Chipping Campden at Old Coombe. They then had two more sons in Chipping Campden, Frederick in 1866 and Albert in 1867. In 1881 they were living in Westington, Chipping Campden and had another son, Joseph. Six of William and Emma's sons were still living with them, with the eldest four following the family tradition by working as shepherds. Also living with them was a granddaughter, Ellen Hedges. Ellen was the daughter of unmarried 'Anna' Hedges, who was probably William's daughter, Fanny Ann. William and Emma continued to live in Westington where William worked as a shepherd. In 1891 two of their sons were still living at home. Fred was working as a general labourer and his son Albert was an agricultural labourer. Ellen was also living with them, now described as their daughter.

Fig. 33. Charlie Hedges

William Hedges' wife, Emma, died at the end of 1900 and by 1901 he was living as a retired shepherd at Westington with his grandson, Charlie, an ordinary agricultural labourer, son of William Hedges' son, William Henry Hedges. However William then went to live at No 1, Sir Baptist Hicks's

Almshouses in Church Street, Chipping Campden where he stayed until his death in 1919. Charlie was later killed in World War I in Loos, France in 1915.

William Hedges daughter, Hannah Hedges, married Robert Newman at Shipston on Stour Warwickshire at the beginning of 1923. She died in the North Cotswold Registration District in 1981.

William Hedges Daughter, Fanny Ann, was probably the 'Anna' who gave birth to a daughter, Ellen, on 20 March 1876. Ellen was living with William Hedges in 1881. In 1903 Ellen married William Jennings, a grocer's traveller and by 1911 they were living at 88 King's Road, Bengeworth, Worcestershire with a son, Maurice, born in Handsworth Staffordshire in 1906. Ellen died in Evesham in March 1971.

William Hedges' son, William Henry Hedges, married Emma James in 1882 in the Shipston on Stour Registration District which included Chipping Campden and by 1891 they were living next door to his father, William Hedges, in Westington with two sons and three daughters where William Henry was working as a cowman.

Fig 34 William Henry Hedges

Figs. 35 & 36. William Henry Hedges' children Ernest Walter and Lily

*Figs. 37 & 38.
William Henry
Hedges' children
Kate and Jane
Jenny*

They continued to live in Westington where in 1901 William Henry was working as a cattleman on a farm. By then his son, Harry, was a farm labourer and they had another son.

William Hedges' son, Frederick Hedges, married Elizabeth Ann Smith from Chipping Campden in 1892. By 1901 they were living at 29 Paul's Houses, Mickelton, where Fred was working as a carter on a farm, with three sons and a daughter, William, Henry, Nora and Harold. In 1911 they were still living at Pike House, Paul's Houses, Campden with another son, Frederick L(e)onard. Fred was still working as a waggoner on a farm and his two eldest sons were labourers on a farm. Frederick Hedges died in March 1942 in the North Cotswold registration district.

William Hedges son, Albert Hedges, married Helena Clara Field, who was born in Clevedon, Somerset, in early 1897 in Aberfan near Merthyr Tydfil . By 1901 they were sharing a house with another family at 4, Cottrell Street, Aberfan, Merthyr Tydfil and had two sons, William H. born about 1898 and Albert G, born about 1899. The family remained in Aberfan and by 1911 they were living at 17 Bryntaf, a terraced house with a dormer window, and Albert was a colliery timberman. His son William only aged 13 was working as a colliery hewer and Helena's mother, Sarah Field, had come to live with them from Somerset. Albert Hedges died in the Merthyr Tydfil registration district in March 1932.

William Hedges son, Joseph Hedges, married Emily Jane Bennett, the daughter of a carpenter from Hackney, in Epsom on 25 December 1896. They settled in Epsom and in 1901 were living in Crimea Cottage near Epsom Common with three daughters; Emma, Edith and Alice, all born in Epsom. Joseph Hedges died there in June 1939.

Joseph Evans

Cecil Sharp visited Joseph Evans on 3 April 1907 in Old Sodbury when Joseph sang him one verse of the song *The Twelve Joys of Mary*, whilst a lady in the village was able to supply the complete words.

Joseph Evans was baptised 2 January 1827 in Beverstone, Gloucestershire. By 1841, aged 13, he was living in Winstone with his parents, Thomas Evans, aged 36, an agricultural labourer and Hannah aged 37 plus his seven siblings, William, Jacob/Jack, Timothy, Thomas, Evan, Jabus and Timothy aged from 15 years to 3 months. All were born in Gloucestershire.

In 1851 the family were still living in Winstone, Gloucestershire. His father, Thomas, was then a shepherd, his mother Hannah, was described as a shepherd's wife born in Beverstone, Gloucestershire, and they had four further children, Able aged 11, Benjamin aged 9, Sarah Ann aged 5 and another child aged 1. Thomas and all the children were born in Winstone. Jacobs was now an agricultural labourer and Jabus a ploughboy. Joseph was not at the family home but he would have been aged approximately 23.

By 1861 Joseph Evans aged 36 was a shepherd living at The Oaks, Sudeley Parish, Gloucestershire with his wife, Elizabeth aged 35, born Winstone, Gloucestershire and children Mary Ann aged 9, a scholar born in Winstone, Gloucestershire, Johana aged 6, a scholar born Sudeley, Gloucestershire,

Thomas aged 5 and Elizabeth aged 2 born in Winstone. He had moved to Berrymans, Stroud (probably near Lypiatt Park) by 1871 and had two of their children living with them: Thomas aged 15, an agricultural labourer, and Eme (prob Emma – see below) aged 7. Thomas was born in Bisley and Eme in Tetbury. The family appears to have moved around Gloucestershire and by 1881 Joseph and Elizabeth were living in Lye Grove, Old Sodbury with Emma/Eme. Also living with them was John Walker aged 29, an under-shepherd born in Old Sodbury. There were no other Evans living in Old Sodbury at the time.

Joseph then remained in Old Sodbury and was noted in censuses as a farm labourer aged 65 in 1891 living in Cotswold Lane, Old Sodbury with his wife Elizabeth, also aged 65 and the couple were still resident there in 1901. Elizabeth was possibly buried in Old Sodbury on 6 November 1904 and a Joseph in Old Sodbury on 22 April 1914.

THOMAS CLAPPEM

Thomas Clappem of 26 Driffield, Cirencester, sang the ballad *The Unquiet Grave* to James Madison Carpenter between 1927 and 1935. He signed his name 'Clappen' in the 1911 census and all family records seem to show that this was the spelling of their surname which they usually used, although Carpenter wrote it as 'Clappem'.

Carpenter noted that he learned this from his mother seventy years ago.

Carpenter referred to Thomas Clappen as a shepherd – his family were longstanding Driffield residents, all agricultural labourers and as such did not have much money. His grandfather, Robert, was born in Driffield in 1785. By 1841 Robert and his wife, Mary Packer from South Cerney, who was 15 years younger than him, were living there with five sons, Thomas born about 1826, Robert born about 1829, John born about 1831(Thomas' father), William born about 1835 and Benjamin born about 1841 plus three daughters, Elizabeth also born about 1826, Sarah born about 1833 and Mary Ann born about 1839. In 1851 they were still living in Driffield and now had their grandson, Henry, living with them. Henry was born about 1845 and in the 1861 census it was stated that he had been born in Cirencester workhouse. Mary's widower father who was a pauper /agricultural labourer was also living with them. John was the eldest child still at home and he, Sarah, William, Mary Ann and Benjamin were all described as agricultural labourers. Benjamin aged 10 was also described as an evening and Sunday scholar with his education being limited to these times as was often the case in those days. All the children had been born in Driffield except Benjamin who had been born in Bentham. *(Figs 39 and 40)*

Figs. 39 & 40

Thomas' father, John Clappen, married Jane Curtis, also born in Driffield, in Driffield Church on 18 September 1857. A year later, Thomas was born and was baptised in Driffield Church on 25 September 1854. In 1861 he was living with his parents in a cottage next to a small grocer's shop in High Street Driffield. His grandparents, Robert and Mary, were living in 'top of village' in Driffield. John and Jane had another son, Charles John born 28 September 1862 in Driffield, and another daughter, Sarah Jane, who died near birth in 1869.

Both John and Jane lived to a good age, John dying in 1913 and Jane in 1917.

Thomas was still living at home in 1871. In 1877 he married Emma Harding who was born in Trowbridge, Wiltshire, and in 1881 he was working as a carter and agricultural labourer living at no 26 cottage in Driffield with Emma and their two daughters: Emma Florence born about 1879 and Sarah Jane born 5 September 1880. His parents, John and Jane, were living in no 17 Cottage Driffield with their son Charles John. Thomas and Emma had another daughter, Emily Harding Clappen, on 3 August 1884.They also had a son, Thomas William born in 1885 who died in 1888. The family were still living in the same cottage in Driffield in 1891. Emily was the only daughter still at home and she was working as a housemaid. By 1911 they were living there on their own. Thomas died in 1937 in the Cirencester registration district.

Thomas's daughter Emma Florence married Henry Hicks from Woolaston, Worcestershire, in the Cirencester registration district at the end of 1904. By 1911 Emma and Henry were living in Cirencester where Henry was working as a groom. They had four sons, Henry born about 1905 in Driffield, William born about 1907 in Cirencester, Reginald born 1908 in Cirencester and Benjamin born 1910 also in Cirencester. All their children were still alive. Also living with them was Henry's widowed mother, Eliza Hicks. Emma had another son, Edward C. Hicks in 1912 and a daughter, Muriel F. Hicks, in 1914.

ROBERT CARPENTER

Like many shepherds the shepherd Robert Carpenter sang about working on the land. He sang *The Pretty Ploughing Boy* to Alfred Williams at Cerney Wick between 1913 and 1916. Alfred Williams noted that Mr Carpenter gained the prize for singing this in a competition held at Kemble Flower Show in the year 1893.

Robert Carpenter's family were originally from Colesbourne. His great-grandfather, Robert Carpenter, and his wife, Esther were living there on the birth of Robert's grandfather James, in 1797. James and his wife Sarah, from Winchcombe, moved to Duntisbourne Abbots where James worked as an agricultural labourer and they were living there with their family, including Robert's father, Thomas, in 1841. Thomas worked as a shepherd and married Hannah who was born in London and they moved to Duntisborne Rouse where Robert Carpenter was born and baptised on 22 December in 1850. Between 1851 and 1861 the family moved to Cote Road, Aston and Cote, Oxfordshire where Thomas was described as an agricultural labourer. By then Robert also had two sisters, Sarah born about 1857 in Beverstone, Gloucestershire and, Mary born 1860 in Sherborne, Gloucestershire.

By 1871 Robert had left home and was working as an agricultural labourer living in Shipton Oliffe village, lodging in the household of Josiah Cross, a shepherd, and his family. In 1876 Robert Carpenter married Ellen Gardiner born in Coates and by 1881 they were living in Colcutt. They had moved around the area and had four children: Charles, age 4 baptised 7 January 1877 in Coates, Fanny E. born about 1878 in Clapton, Alice M. born 1880 in Farmington and Susannah born in 1881 in Coln St Dennis. The family continued to move around and in 1891 they were living in Ewen Road, Kemble. They then had two more children: Walter G. born about 1884 in Preston, Gloucestershire and John born about 1887 in Sapperton. Robert was still working as a shepherd and his son, Charles, was a farm labourer. By 1901 the family had moved to Number 13, Driffield. Whilst Robert continued to work as a shepherd, his son, Walter, was a hall boy (domestic) and his son John was a farm labourer. These were the only two of his children still living at home. Charles, his son, had moved to live with his married sister, Alice in Corston, Wiltshire, and was out of work.

Robert's health obviously deteriorated after this as in 1911 he was a patient in Gloucester County Lunatic Asylum. He was still married and described as a farm labourer (shepherd). His wife, Ellen, was living at Poulton, and listed as head of the family and at age 62 was working as a farm labourer and living with her grandson, Robert Watts, age 7, born in Driffield, She had been married for 26 years and had six children all still living. Despite Robert's health, he was to sing to Alfred Williams after this date. Robert Carpenter died of heart failure at the end of 1920 at the Stableton Institution in Bristol, the former workhouse which was mainly used for people with mental problems.

Robert Carpenter's son, John Thomas Carpenter, married Agnes Dyon on 3 April 1909 in Malmesbury and in 1911 was living at 3, Quenington Rd, Quarry Farm, Poulton with his wife and their one year old son, Reginald, who was born in Poulton on 24 January 1910. By 1920 they had moved to Caudwell, Malmesbury, and had another son, Elwin Frederick born 7 November 1915. John worked as an auxiliary postman but was then called up in 1915.

Robert Carpenter's daughter, Fanny Elizabeth Carpenter, married George Smith, a labourer from Coln St Dennis, in 1901, had one daughter and subsequently died in Cirencester Cottage Hospital on 31 January 1921.

Robert Carpenter's daughter, Alice Carpenter, married Ernest James Watts, a groom and son of a labourer, on 4 April 1903. They lived in Corston, Wiltshire where Alice had a daughter, Mabel, in 1906 and three sons, Robert, born 1904, Leslie born 1907 and Cecil born 1910 and probably died in Bristol in 1930.

Robert Carpenter's daughter, Susannah Carpenter, was married twice, firstly to Thomas Painter, a labourer, at Driffield on 21 November 1904 and then after she was widowed to Maurice Eldridge, a shepherd whose wife had died the previous year, on 17 November 1915 in Preston, Glos.

CHARLES PHELPS

Sarah Phelps, wife of the shepherd and agricultural labourer, Charles Phelps, of 7, Council Houses, Avening sang the courting songs *The Broomfield Hill* and *The Diamond Token,* the ballads *The Outlandish Knight* and *The Unquiet Grave,* the well-known song *The Fox* and a nonsense song *There Was an Old Woman* to James Madison Carpenter sometime between 1927 and 1935. Carpenter noted that her mother used to sing to the children. Charles Phelps, Sarah's husband, also sang *John Barleycorn* to James Madison Carpenter. For more information about this family see Mill Workers below.

ROBERT WAKEFIELD

Percy Grainger visited Mr R. Wakefield in Winchcombe Workhouse on 5 April 1908 when he sang *The Constant Farmer's Son*.

Robert Wakefield was born in 1839 in Calmesden near North Cerney into a family of shepherds. He was the son of James Wakefield, a shepherd born in 1791 in North Cerney, the son of William and Esther Wakefield. In 1841 James and his wife, Mary, who was born in Chedworth, were living in Coates with two other sons, Henry born about 1833 and Charles born about 1836 plus four daughters, Harriett born about 1826, Mary Ann born about 1829, Elizabeth born about

1831 and Emma born about 1838. James' parents were also living with them but William died in 1847. In 1851 Robert was living at home in North Cerney and his parents had another daughter, Ellen, born about 1846.

By 1861 he had left home and was working as a shepherd and lodging with a shepherd, Henry Gleed, in Coalpits, Rumstone (near Chepstow). His parents were still living in North Cerney where his father was working as a shepherd. All their children had left home but they had taken in two lodgers who were agricultural labourers.

James Wakefield, Robert's father, died in 1869. Robert Wakefield married Harriet Brunsdon in Chedworth on 29 July 1866 and by 1871 they were living in Newport Cottage, Chedworth, where Robert was working as an agricultural labourer, with Harriet's son William Brunsdon, born about 1864 before she was married, and their three children, Charles born about 1867, James, born about 1868 and Henry, born about 1871. Robert and Harriet had four more daughters before 1881, Mary Elizabeth (also known as Emily Elizabeth) born 1873, Sarah Ann born about 1876, Eunice born about 1878 and Alice born 1880. About 1880 Robert and Harriet moved to North Cerney where Robert continued working as a shepherd. At the time of the 1881 Census Harriet's son, William, was not in the house and his sons Charles and James were working as agricultural labourers. Before 1891 they had again moved to Colcutt Peak Farm, Coln St Dennis where Robert and his son, Henry, were working as agricultural labourers as was Harriet's son, William, who was again in the household and was given the surname Wakefield. The only other child still at home in 1891 was Alice. Robert's wife, Harriet, died in 1899 and by 1901 Robert had moved in with his daughter, Alice, and her family in Guiting Power. He was stated to be a farm labourer at that time although at the time of his daughter, Sarah Ann's, wedding in 1903 his occupation was given as a shepherd. He was admitted to Winchcombe Workhouse on 13 April 1905 where he remained until 25 July 1905 but was discharged from there on 25 July 1906. He was back in the workhouse by July 1907 where he remained until 3 February 1911 when he left the workhouse to move in with his daughter, Sarah Ann, and her family in Withington. Robert Wakefield died in 1918 in the Northleach registration district. At least two of his sons also became shepherds and one of his daughters also married a shepherd.

MILL WORKERS

The wool from Cotswold Sheep led to the growth in woollen mills which employed large numbers of people in Gloucestershire. One singer whose family were associated with shepherding and the woollen industry was **Charles Phelps** who sang the drinking song *John Barleycorn* to James Madison Carpenter between 1927 and 1935. The Phelps family lived in the village of Bisley for many generations. One family tree on *www.ancestry.com* traces them there back to 1500, with ten generations of Charles Phelps' family having been born in Bisley. Many of these ancestors would have originally worked in the cottage woollen industry but the arrival of mill machinery in 1838 brought an abrupt end to the cottage weaving industry in Bisley. In 1837 the Rector of Bisley wrote that 'In consequence of the failure of work since the autumn of last year, the resources of very many families are entirely exhausted, and almost all are suffering extreme Privations... and though benevolent persons have rendered some aid, still it is certain and can be proved, if required, that many pass whole days without food.' Charles' great-grandfather, Richard Phelps, who had been born in Bisley moved to Rodmarton and was living there in 1841 next door to his son, William,

Charles' grandfather, and his family, both working then as agricultural labourers.

Charles' father, Thomas Phelps, was baptised on 18 February 1820 in Rodmarton, the eldest of probably seven children. In 1843 he married Mary Luker, who was born in Cherington, in the Tetbury registration district which included Avening. By 1851 they were living in Nagshead, Avening with Thomas' brother, Henry, and two children, William born 1847 and Jane born 1849. Thomas and Henry were both working as agricultural labourers. By 1861 they were still living in Nagshead, Avening where Thomas was working as an agricultural labourer. Henry was no longer living with them but they had four more children, Hannah born 1853, another William born 1855 (presumably the first William had died), Joseph born 1858 and Harriet born 1860, all born in Avening. Thomas and his daughter, Elizabeth, were both working as agricultural labourers. Charles Phelps was baptised in Avening on 3 January 1864, apparently the youngest son of Thomas and Mary Phelps.

By 1871 the family were again associated with the cloth industry. Charles was living at home in Nagshead, Avening and although his father and two brothers, William and Joseph, were working as agricultural labourers, his two eldest sisters, Jane and Hannah were both working in a silk factory and his other sister, Harriet, was a scholar, as was he. By 1881 Charles was still living at home at Nagshead, Avening, and had started working as an agricultural labourer as were his father, mother, brother, William, and sister, Harriet. The woollen industry still supported the Phelps family however as his other sibling still living at home, Jane, was working as a mill hand. And in 1886 Charles married **Sarah** Ockwell from Cherington, his mother's birthplace who had been working as a cloth cutter. Sarah Ockwell was the daughter of Alfred and Harriet Ockwell, agricultural labourers, one of at least ten children. She was born in Cherington in 1866 and in 1881 was living at home working as a cloth cutter. Sarah was also a singer (see in Chapter 2 'Occupations' above for a list of her songs).

Sarah Ockwell was the daughter of Alfred and Harriet Ockwell, agricultural labourers, one of at least ten children. She was born in Cherington in 1866 and in 1881 was living at home working as a cloth cutter. Charles' father, Thomas Phelps, died in 1888 and by 1891 Charles and Sarah Phelps were living in Cherington village, where Charles was working as a farm labourer. They had ten children, Elsie born 1887, Fred born abut 1889, Lucy born 1890, Arthur born 1893, Norah born 1896, Beatrice born 1899, Linda born 1901, Bertram born 1904, Norman born 1906 and Harry born 1908. In 1901 and 1911 Charles and Sarah were still living in Cherington and in 1911 Charles was working there as a shepherd. Living next door to them was Sarah's brother, Ralph Ockwell aged 32, and his family, a horse/keeper on a farm. Charles Phelps died in March 1941 in the Cirencester registration district.

Charles' Children

Charles' son Bertram married and had 3 daughters, according to a family tree on Ancestry.com.

Bertram's wife was Cecilia May Chipp, 1915 – 1994, and his daughters were Brenda E. Phelps born 1943 and Nina D. Phelps born 1948.

Charlie's daughter Linda Phelps married Charles Hawkins and had a daughter and a son, Charles Frederick M. Hawkins 1926 – 1987. The daughter married and had 2 daughters and a son. Both of these daughters married and one had a daughter and a son, the other had 2 daughters.

Another family associated with the mill industry was that of singer George Hill of Dursley. Further details of his family can be found in the Chapter on Singers of Comic Songs.

The Shepherds' Song

1. We shep-herds are the best of men, That e'er trod Eng—lish ground; When we come to an ale-house We va-lue not a crown. We spend our mon-ey free-ly, We pay be-fore— we go; - - - There's no ale on— the wolds Where— the stor-my winds— do blow, We

spend our mon-ey free-ly, We pay be-fore— we go—

Chorus

There's no ale on— the wolds Where— the stor-my winds— do blow

1. We shepherds are the best of men,
   That e'er trod English ground;
   When we come to an alehouse
   We value not a crown.
   We spend our money freely,
   We pay before we go;
   There's no ale on the wolds
   Where the stormy winds do blow
   Chorus.--We spend, &c

2. A man that is a shepherd
   Does need a valiant heart,
   He must not be faint-hearted,
   But boldly do his part.
   He must not be faint-hearted,
   Be it rain, or frost, or snow,
   With no ale on the wolds
   Where the stormy winds do blow.
   Chorus.--He must not, etc.

3. When I kept sheep on Blockley Hills
   It made my heart to ache
   To see the ewes hang out their tongues
   And hear the lambs to bleat;
   Then I plucked up my courage
   And o'er the hills did go,
   And penned them in the fold
   While the stormy winds do blow.
   Chorus.--The I plucked up, etc.

4. As soon as I had folded them
   I turned me back in haste
   Unto a jovial company
   Good liquor for to taste;
   For drink and jovial company
   They are my heart's delight,
   Whilst my sheep lie asleep
   All the fore-part of the night.
   Chorus.--For drink and jovial company, etc.

Source: Published in "English County Songs" by Broadwood and Fuller Maitland (1893), with the note
"From FF. Scarlett Potter, Esq., Halford, Shipton-on-Stour" and the following explanation "The
first verse was taken from the recitation of an old lady born at Stoke, Gloucestershire, in 1793:
The remaining verses were recovered from Thomas Coldicote, shepherd, of Ebrington,
Gloucestershire. Blockley, referred to in verse 3, is in the parish adjoining Ebrington."

©Gloucestershire Traditions

John Barleycorn

1. There was three men came from the west, a scheme all for to try. And there they made a vow and swore, John Bar - - ley - - corn should

(Chorus)

die. To me right fol lo lol, ti - ddy fol dol, to me right fol lol I

dee. And how they sar'd (i) John Bar - ley - corn, they sar'd him bi - tter - - ly.

(i) served

2. They ploughed him in a furrow deep
With clods upon his head.
And how they did rejoice and sing,
John Barleycorn is dead.

3. He laid there for a very long time
Till the rain from heaven did fall,
And Barleycorn sprung up again
And soon surprised them all.

4. They hired men with scythes so sharp
To cut him off at knee
And so they sar'd John Barleycorn
They sar'd him bitterly.

5. They hired men with picks so sharp
To stab him in the heart
And the carter sar'd him worse than that
For they bound him to a cart.

6. They hauled him round and
round the ground
Till they came to a barn
And there they made a mow of him
To keep him from all harm.

7. They hired men with crabsticks hard
To byet ["beat"] him flesh from bones
And the millard [sic]
sar'd 'n ["him"] worse than that
And 'un ground ["him" = he] 'n
between two stwuns ["stones"].

Source: Sung by Charles Phelps, 7 Council Houses, Avening. Learnt as a lad.
Collected by James Madison Carpenter between 1927 and 1935.

3

SINGERS IN THE WORKHOUSE

With no old age pension or savings, many labourers and workers on the land ended up in the workhouse. This was fertile ground for the folk song collectors who wanted to know what songs and tunes were known by the more elderly members of the population whose memories went back the furthest. Cecil Sharp and Percy Grainger in particular heard many interesting songs in the workhouse.

Why were people in the workhouse? In the nineteenth Century, no official support system or benefits were available for those who were unemployed, elderly, sick or disabled. People had to work to earn money, and so if they were unable to for any reason, they had no means of paying rent or buying food. Before 1834 poor relief was the responsibility of individual parishes. In 1832 the government set up a Royal Commission to investigate the existing system and make recommendations for changes. The solution seemed to be to reduce the number of people claiming relief and to abolish 'outdoor relief' – the practice of supporting people in their own homes. Anyone not able to support themselves would be cared for in a workhouse. Under the provisions of the Poor Law Amendment Act, 1834, the whole of England and Wales was divided into Poor Law Unions – there were about 650 in all – administered by an elected Board of Guardians. Each union provided a single workhouse to accommodate anyone not able to support themselves. The workhouse was intended to be so unpleasant that people would either find employment or turn to a charity or their family for support.[17] Parishes (like council wards) joined funds in order to build a workhouse – a place for the impoverished and destitute to live and work. Several parishes were grouped together into Unions, so that many of the establishments were known as union workhouses. Each union was responsible for providing a central workhouse for its member parishes, where the paupers were separated and allocated to the appropriate ward for their category: boys under 14, able-bodied men between 14 and 60, men over 60, girls under 14, able-bodied women between 14 and 60, and women over 60.

Many inmates were allocated tasks in the workhouse such as caring for the sick – they had to have permission to go out but were free to leave whenever they wished after giving reasonable notice, generally considered to be three hours.[18]

As the 19th century wore on, workhouses increasingly became refuges for the elderly, infirm and sick rather than the able-bodied poor, and in 1929 legislation was passed to allow local authorities to take over workhouse infirmaries as municipal hospitals.

Men and women were separated, as were the able-bodied and infirm, which meant that families were separated, some never to be reunited. Those who were able to work did so for their bed and board. Women took on domestic chores such as cooking, laundry and sewing, while men performed physical labour, usually stone breaking, oakum picking or bone crushing. Many children were born into workhouse life, as unmarried mothers were cast out from society and forced to seek shelter there. Conditions were basic: parents and children were permitted to meet briefly on a daily basis, or on Sundays.

Inmates ate simple fare in a large communal dining hall, and were compelled to take regular, supervised baths.[19]

The general attitude towards the poor was one of disdain, and the belief that they deserved their unfortunate status was widely held. Conditions in the workhouses were deliberately basic to act as a deterrent, and to discourage people seeking an 'easy' option. It was meant as a last resort solution to poverty, providing shelter, clothing and food. Only the most desperate people turned to the workhouses for help. Discipline was strictly enforced; for minor offences such as swearing or feigning sickness the 'disorderly' could have their diet restricted for up to 48 hours. For more serious offences such as insubordination or violent behaviour the 'refractory' could be confined for up to 24 hours.

Meals were basic at best. Cheap, filling food such as gruel (a thick porridge-like sludge), bread and cheese, broth, rice, milk, and potatoes were most common. The workhouses were strictly run, with many rules which were to be adhered to at all times, with consequences for those who flouted them. Jobs were found for the inmates, either inside the workhouse to maintain the building and the residents, or sent out as cheap labour to fund the workhouse. The institutions had infirmaries for the sick, and employed some of the more adept inmates as nurses. Many workhouses developed and became hospitals in the 20th century.

A typical example of the singers found in workhouses was **Peter Gill** of Sheepscombe who ended up in the **Stroud Union workhouse** where he was visited by the song collector Cecil Sharp on 2 April 1912 when he sang the carols *Christ Came to Christmas* and *The Moon Shines Bright,* and country songs *Dabbling in the Dew* and *Shepherds are the Best of Men.*

Peter Gill's father, Levi Gill, was born about 1799 in Sheepscombe. His wife was Ann, born about 1797 also in Sheepscombe. Levi was a labourer who in 1820 was living in a cottage which used to stand on the hillside above Greycot, as a tenant of Daniel Gill (possibly a relation). They had at least five children: Joseph and Andrew, twins, born in 1826, Priscilla born in 1827, Felix born in 1831 and Peter, born in 1835/6. His age was given in the 1841 Census as 5. In other censuses his age is variable as was often the case with people in those days. He informed Cecil Sharp that he was 83 in 1912, older than his correct age.

Peter married Sarah Ann Gibbons, a shoemaker's daughter, in Sheepscombe in 1857. Both were living in Sheepscombe at the time.

In 1861 Peter and Sarah, both aged 26, were living in Sheepscombe Village with their children Albert aged 3 and Alfred aged 1. Also living with them was Peter's father Levi, then aged 62, following his wife's death in 1854. Peter, Sarah and Levi were agricultural labourers and Albert was a scholar. All the family except Sarah Ann were born in Sheepscombe whereas Sarah was born in Siddington.

By 1871 Peter and Sarah were still living in Sheepscombe with their son, Albert, now aged 13 but they also then had Frederick aged 11, George aged 8, Mary aged 7, Emily aged 3 and Elizabeth J. aged 11 months. Another child, Henry had died in 1866, making a total of eight known children. Peter's father, Levi, aged 73 was also still living with them. Levi, Peter, Sarah, Albert and Frederick were all agricultural labourers and the younger children were scholars.

Peter's father, Levi Gill was buried 27 November 1879 aged 81 in Sheepscombe. In 1881 Peter and Sarah were still in Sheepscombe. The children remaining at home with them were Frederick aged 21, Mary aged 17, Emily aged 13 and Elizabeth aged 10. Frederick was an agricultural labourer, Mary was a general servant and the 2 youngest children were scholars. All the family except for Sarah were born in Sheepscombe.

In 1891 Peter Gill was living in Magpie Bottom, Sheepscombe, employed as an agricultural labourer, with his wife, Sarah, then 56. Two of their daughters were still at home – Mary aged 27 and Elizabeth J. aged 20. Both daughters were domestic servants.

By 1901 after the death of Sarah in 1894 aged 60 Peter, as an agricultural labourer, was a boarder at Bramble Farm, Cranham held by John Larner, a farm shepherd born in Whittington, and Mary Larner his wife who was born in Syde. His fortune went downhill and by 1911 aged 77 as a widowed farm labourer Peter was an inmate at Stroud Union Workhouse, Bisley Road, Stroud where he was recorded by Cecil Sharp.

Peter therefore had eight children between 1857 and 1870. Most went to Sheepscombe school and all seem to have been agricultural labourers or servants with large families who would have found it difficult to support their elderly father.

Peter Gill died on 17 January 1917 aged 80 in Stroud Union Workhouse and was buried at Sheepscombe on 22 January 1917.

Following the Poor Law Amendment Act of 1834, Stroud Union workhouse was built in 1837 to the north side of Bisley Road and covered 37,000 square feet. It was managed by a Board of 31 Guardians. The Stroud Union consisted of the parishes of Avening, Bisley, Cranham, Horsley, Minchinhampton, Miserden, Painswick, Pitchcombe, Randwick, Rodborough, Kings Stanley, Leonard Stanley, Stonehouse, Stroud and Woodchester.

The inmates of Stroud Workhouse were considered luckier than others elsewhere in the country, but conditions were still far from luxurious. It was a shameful place to be sent, as Howard Beard describes in his book, *Around Stroud*. He wrote, *'My great-grandfather suffered from the delusions which today we might associate with Alzheimer's disease.'* This contributed to his removal in the 1920s to Stroud workhouse, '*When he died there shortly afterwards, his death certificate gave his residence as 1, Bisley Road and the informant of his decease (one of the staff) as The Occupier, 1, Bisley Road. No-one, surely, was really fooled by such reluctance to acknowledge that he died in the workhouse.*' [20]

Although workhouses were supposed to be terrible places, the workhouse in Bisley Old Road was one of the most up to date and modern. The old people living there were treated fairly well but it took a great deal of money to keep all the occupants fed for one year.

Another important musician and source of traditional music was 72-year old **John Mason**, whom Cecil J Sharp met in **Stow-on-the-Wold Workhouse** on several occasions from 1907 onwards.

Fig. 41. John Mason
(Photo: Vaughan Williams Memorial Library)

The Stow-on-the-Wold union workhouse was built in 1836 at a site to the north-east of the town, on what became known as Union Street. Stow-On-The-Wold Poor Law Union was formed on 25th January 1836. Its operation was overseen by an elected Board of Guardians, 30 in number, representing its 28 constituent parishes as listed below (figures in brackets indicate numbers of Guardians if more than one):

County of Gloucester: Adlestrop, Great Barrington,
   Bledington, Bourton-on-the-Water (2), Broadwell,
   Clapton, Condicote, Donnington, Eyford, Icomb,
   Church Icomb, Longborough, Maugersbury,
   Naunton, Notgrove, Oddington, Great Rissington,
   Little Rissington, Wick Rissington, Sezincote, Lower
   Slaughter, Upper Slaughter, Stow-on-the-Wold (2),
   Lower Swell, Upper Swell, Westcote.

County of Worcester: Daylesford, Evenlode.

The song collector Cecil Sharp visited John Mason on
a number of occasions: 27-28 March and 2-3 August 1907,
29 July, 2 August and 18 August 1909 and 21-22 June 1912.
Mason had played fiddle for the Sherborne Morris dancers
(and possibly others) and, as well as providing Sharp with
a number of tunes, he volunteered the address of William
Hathaway in Cheltenham, the location of Sherborne Morris's
George Simpson near Didcot and gave other leads towards
participants in the Longborough, Bledington and Oddington
morris sets. Curiously, many of the tunes which Mason
described as 'Morris Dance' are not generally known as such.
He also sang the songs *Greensleeves* and *The Shepherdess* to Cecil
Sharp on his visit on 28 March 1907. He was also visited by
other collectors: one W. H. Hunt collected the lengthy Icombe
Mummers play from him, noting that the mummers used to
sing the song *The Golden Glove* at the end of the play. This play
was published in the Antiquary in 1913 quoting the Notes and
Queries version of the Evesham Journal. The Morris dance
collector Clive Carey also visited him and noted several Morris
tunes. One can assume he was allowed to keep his fiddle with
him in the workhouse.

   As well as fiddle, Mason played clarinet, flute and
concertina. He was also visited by Mary Neal and Clive Carey

shortly before he died and they noted several of the tunes he had previously played for Sharp. Twenty two of John Mason's tunes are included on the website at www.glostrad.com.

John Mason was born in Icomb and was baptised there on 3 August 1834, the son of Thomas and Charlotte Mason, formerly Robins. The portion of the parish known as Church Icomb was in Worcestershire until 1844 but when John Mason was 10 years old there was a boundary change and Church Icomb became part of Gloucestershire to join the portion of the parish known as Westward Icomb which had always been in Gloucestershire. John Mason's father, Thomas Mason was also born in Icomb and baptised there on 22 February 1789, the son of William Mason. In 1841 John Mason was living in Icomb, then in Worcestershire, with his father, Thomas, an agricultural labourer and his older brother, Joseph, also an agricultural labourer and two older sisters, Eliza and Ann. His father, Thomas, died and was buried in Icomb on 1 June 1849 whereupon he and his mother, Charlotte, went to live with his sister, Ann, and her husband, John Wilkes, an agricultural labourer from Idbury, in Icomb. John Mason was working there in 1851 as an agricultural labourer and Charlotte and Ann as laundresses. John Mason married Hannah Stayte from Bledington in Icomb on 19 April 1863. By 1871 they were living in Church Icomb with five children: Thomas Edward Stayt Mason born 1864, Frederick William born 1865, John Edwin Mason born 1867, Louisa Mason born 1869 and Mary M. Mason born 1871. John Mason was working as a labourer as he was also in 1881 when the family were still living in Church Icomb. John's son, Thomas, was then working as an undercarter, his son, Frederick was an errand boy and John's son, John, was a stable boy. John and Hannah also subsequently had five more children: Ada born 1873, Emma born 1875, Eva born 1877 and twins, William and Sarah J., born 1880. John

Mason's wife, Hannah, died in 1882 aged 40 and by 1891 John was living on his own in Church Icomb, still working as an agricultural labourer as he was also in 1901. By 1907 John Mason had entered Stow on the Wold Workhouse where he was visited by the folk collectors and he died there in 1912.

JOHN MASON'S CHILDREN

Most of John Mason's children left to work in London and worked variously as a hotel waiter, coachman and groom, parlour maid, butler and domestic servant, none of whom would have been earning very much money to support their father.

The information which Mason provided to Cecil Sharp contributed greatly to the recovery of the Cotswold Morris traditions which are performed today.

The site of **Winchcombe workhouse** moved several times. Firstly it was located in Cowl Lane followed by Silk Mill Lane and then Back Lane in Winchcombe.

The Winchcombe Union Workhouse (seen here in 1904) extended from Gloucester Street to Langley Road on the site now occupied by a modern terrace, the Day Centre and sheltered housing. It has been demolished, but much of its high solid stone boundary wall still remains.

Fig. 42. The Winchcomb Union Workhouse.
(Photo: Winchcombe Folk and Police Museum)

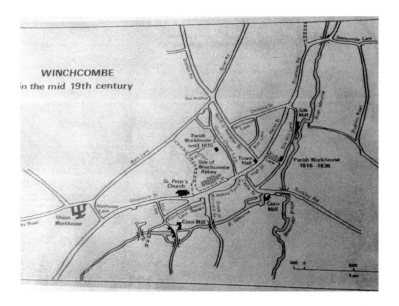

Fig. 43. Winchcombe in the 19th century showing the location of the workhouse – bottom left

Eliza Wedgwood (of the Wedgwood pottery family) was the daughter of the vicar of Dumbleton and took an interest in the local people and, in particular, their songs.[21] On New Year's Day 1908 she and a friend Elena Rathbone who was a member of the Folk Song Society, visited the workhouse to record songs from the singers there. Following their success on this visit they encouraged the collectors Percy Grainger and Cecil Sharp to record many singers at Winchcombe workhouse. Workhouse records show that Eliza Wedgwood and her friends entertained the inmates at Christmas and invited some of the women to her house.

Many people did not live permanently in the workhouse but went in and out as their circumstances dictated. One such person was **George 'Daddy' Lane**.

Percy Grainger visited George 'Daddy' Lane aged 83 at Winchcombe workhouse on 5 April 1908 when he sang into

Fig. 44. Phonograph as used by collector Percy Grainger to collect songs from George 'Daddy' Lane

Percy Grainger's phonograph *The Banks of Sweet Dundee, Claudy Banks, High Germany, The Irish Girl, The Nightingale Sings, Shepherd's Song, Susan My Dear, 'Twas Early, Early All In The Spring, The Valiant Munroe* and *The Wraggle Taggle Gypsies.* Also Grainger returned on 24 August 1908 when George sang him *We Shepherds Are The Best Of Men.* Grainger later noted that George had died before his return to the Workhouse on 31 July 1909.

George Lane was born in Alston, variously in Worcestershire and Gloucestershire, in 1825, where he was christened on 24 April of the same year, the son of Thomas and Margaret Lane born about 1785 and 1786 respectively.

In 1841 aged 15 George was living in Alstone with his parents, Thomas and Margaret. Thomas was an agricultural labourer. He married Caroline Redding in October 1848 in Winchcombe. Caroline was born in Wormington in about 1824. By 1851 he was still living in Alstone but now working as an agricultural labourer living with Caroline and his one-year old son, Charles. In 1861 he was living at Alstone Farm, working as an agricultural labourer with his mother, his wife and their 5 children: Charles aged 11, a farm labourer, Lucia aged 9, Emma aged 7, William aged 5 and Joseph aged 2. All the children were born in Alstone. They had another daughter, Mary Ann, about 1867. By 1861 George was still living in Alstone with his wife and his son Joseph, all working as agricultural labourers, and another three children: George aged 9, Hurbert aged 6 and Emma aged 4, all born in Alstone. By 1881 aged 56 George was a carter living in a house on a farm in Alstone with his wife and sons: Joseph and Herbert, agricultural labourers, and George, a blacksmith journeyman. At the time of the 1891 Census he and his wife were living in Alstone Fields, Gloucestershire. Staying with them was their son William's daughter, Florence aged 11, born in Hinton, Worcestershire. Both were working as farm labourers.

George's wife, Caroline, died aged 65 at the end of 1892 in Winchcombe registration district and at age 77 in 1901 George was still described as an agricultural labourer and was living in Alstone with his granddaughter, Annie Lane, who was single and aged 23 born in 'Didcote', Glos (probably Hidcote).

Sometimes inmates managed to leave the workhouse if they found work or had relatives who could support them but they often ended up readmitted. George Lane was admitted to Winchcombe Workhouse on 30 December 1902. He was discharged 6 April 1903 but was back in on 16 April. He was discharged again on 30 April 1903 but was readmitted the following day. He then stayed in the workhouse until 4 June 1904 and around January 1904 requested leave to go to his son's for a few days. He was discharged from the workhouse on 4 June 1904 but was back again on 28 June 1904. He then stayed there until 29 August 1904 but was readmitted on 5 September 1904 when the Workhouse Master commented:' *I beg to report that inmate George Lane was readmitted on the 5th Instant, he had upwards of £2.0.0 in his possession.*' He then remained in the workhouse until 15 July 1905 but returned on 1 August 1905 and remained there until his death on 19 December 1908 between Percy Grainger's two visits to Winchcombe workhouse in 1908 and 1909. His granddaughter, Annie, had married in 1904 probably to William George Lane.

GEORGE'S CHILDREN

George's eldest son, Charles, was born in Alstone, then in Worcestershire, and at age 11 was noted as a farm labourer. Charles married Ann Hewins in 1876 in the Winchcombe registration district. In 1881 they were living in Greet where Charles was a carter at a flour mill. They had two daughters, Edith A.(Ann or Austin) born about 1878 and Bertha Minnie born 1880, both in Greet. By 1891 they had moved to Herefordshire and were living at Silverstones, Hope Mansel, in Herefordshire, where Charles was a farm bailiff and his wife was working as a dairywoman.

By 1901 Charles was still in Herefordshire and was one of four families living at The Dam, Walford Village, Herefordshire where he was working as a groom and gardener. He died in the Ross on Wye registration district in 1909.

Charles' daughter, Edith, was working as a housemaid for a solicitor in East Court, Charlton Kings in 1901. She probably had a short marriage around 1910 as by 1911 she was described as a widow. She then married George William Broughton and they had one daughter, Phyllis, who was born in 1918 in Glamorganshire. Phyllis married Neville Martin Lane in 1942. They had one child. Neville died in East Glamorgan in 1966 and Phyllis died in 2011 in Aberystwyth.

Fig. 45. Phyllis Broughton

Fig. 46. Neville Martin Lane

Charles' daughter, Bertha Minnie, married William Edward Green, a colliery shoeing smith in 1902. They had ten children: Sadie born in Aberfan, Ada, born 1903 in Aberfan , Minnie born 1904/5 in Aberfan, Margaret Ann born 1905 in Aberfan, Edward Charles born 1909 in Aberfan, Thomas born 1910, Morfydd born 1912, Wyndham born 1913, Maldwyn born 1915, Albert and Ralph born 1916, all in Merthyr registration district, and Thomas. In 1911 Ada was living at 38 Bryntaf Aberfan as housemaid to a retired army officer. She married Reg Mathieson in 1924. They had two sons, Roy and Terry. She died in London in 1973. Minnie married William Richard Cartwright in 1929. They had one son, Richard T. Cartwright, who died shortly after birth and one further son and a daughter. Minnie died in 1998 in Merthyr. Margaret Ann (Maggie) married William Henry Carpenter and had one son. Margaret died in Croydon in 1994 and her husband in 1977. Edward Charles married Theresa MacLauchlan. Thomas died in 1978 in Londonderry. Wyndham died in 1999 in Pontypridd. Maldwyn was married in 1956 and died in Merthyr in 1990. Albert Ralph died in Pontypridd in 1992.

George's son William was born in 1856. He and his wife, Mary, had two daughters: Ann Maude born about 1878 and Florence Ellen born 1880. Ann may have married Alfred J. Belcher in 1895 and lived in Hailes Street,Winchcombe in

1901. If so, they had two daughters. Mabel A. E. born 1897, Gertrude K. born 1899 and a son, Albert J., born 1900.

George's son, Joseph, an agricultural labourer was born in 1858 and married twice; firstly in 1888 to Lucy Russell Peart, the daughter of his next door neighbour, a grocer and farmer. They had one daughter, Thirza in 1890/91. Secondly he married Eliza Hale in 1893. They had two children, Annie, born about 1895 and Louie born 1897. This may be the Annie whom George Lane was living with in 1901.

George's son, George was a blacksmith journeyman.

The demand for Cotswold stone has always been great and in Winchcombe workhouse we also find people who had been quarryman as well as turning their hand to agricultural labour. One such person was **William Martin**, an agricultural labourer, quarry worker and carter.

William Martin came from an old-established Temple Guiting family. His great-grandparents, Samuel and Elizabeth were living there from at least 1762 from which date seven of their children including William's grandfather, Nathaniel, were baptised in Temple Guiting church. In 1861 William was living at home in Temple Guiting. He, his father and brother, Edwin, were all working as agricultural labourers. His sisters, Hannah, Emma and Sarah were also at home. William's father, George Martin died and was buried in Temple Guiting in February 1865. By 1871 William and his brother, Edwin, were both working as agricultural labourers and living with his mother, Dinah, who was stated to be a pauper in Temple Guiting. In 1881 William was still unmarried and living in Temple Guiting with his mother and working as an agricultural labourer. William continued to live with his mother in Temple Guiting and by 1891 he was a quarry worker. William's mother, Dinah Martin, died in 1899 and by 1901 he was living on his own in Kineton, working as a carter. With no children to support him, William Martin was admitted to Winchcombe Union (Workhouse) on 18 June 1902 and was still there in February 1912 when he was visited by Eliza Wedgwood and sang her *Lost Lady Found* and the *Spotted Cow*. William Martin died in 1922 in Winchcombe.

Men and women could both end up in the workhouse. One woman workhouse inmate who was a prolific singer was **Mrs. Mary Anne Roberts**, a labourer and labourer's wife.

Eliza Wedgwood, Cecil Sharp and Percy Grainger visited Mary Ann Roberts in Winchcombe Workhouse. Miss Wedgwood visited her on 24 April 1908 and stated that she was aged 77 *'and is very gone in the head'*.

Mary Ann's mother, Mary Haines, was born in Fladbury, Worcestershire in about 1794 and by 1841, aged 7 Mary Ann was living in Alderton with her parents, John, aged 35, an agricultural labourer from Bricklehampton, Worcestershire, and Mary, also aged 35, and her siblings.

In 1881 Mary Ann's husband, William, aged 41 was living in Great Washbourne with his children: Walter aged 19, an agricultural labourer, Mary aged 17 of no occupation, Jessie aged 11 and James aged 5, both scholars. All the family except James were born in Ashchurch. Mary Ann was not in the house but a Mary Ann Roberts was in Winchcombe workhouse, an' imbecile' aged 45, wife of an agricultural labourer, born in Moore, Worcestershire so by that date she had succumbed to mental illness. There is an Upper Moor and Lower Moor near Fladbury. By 1891 Mary Ann was out of the workhouse and aged 61 was living in the School House, Beckford, with her husband William aged 51, an agricultural labourer, with their daughter, Jessie, aged 21, a general servant born in Aston on Carrant and their son, James aged 16, born in Great Washbourne, also an agricultural labourer. On 20 January

1908 she was readmitted to Winchcombe Union workhouse and was refused a leave of absence on 23 May 1908 but was referred to examination by the medical officer. She remained there until 4 October 1910 when she was certified insane and removed to the asylum. It is not clear when she died.

Despite her illness, Mary Ann was able to give several complete songs to folk song collectors. Mary Ann Roberts sang Eliza Wedgwood the ballad *Lord Lovel*, courting songs *Betsy the Milkmaid or the Rich Bristol Squire* and *The Young Fisherman* and a religious song *Today You May be Alive God (sic) man*. Eliza Wedgwood only noted the words of these songs. In April 1909, Cecil Sharp obtained from her versions of *Green Brooms, The [Bold] Fisherman, Lord Lovel* and *The Cherry Tree Carol*, the latter learnt from her mother. The collector Percy Grainger subsequently also visited her in July 1909 when he collected the same songs as Sharp had found, plus *Today you may be Alive God [sic] man, I Lived with my Grandmother*, and *The Rich Bristol Squire*.

Married couples were sometimes both admitted together to the workhouse. William and Ann Shepherd were one such couple.

William 'Daddy' Shepherd was baptised in Stow on the Wold on 21 July 1816, the son of Thomas Shepherd, a slater, and his wife, Hannah. By 1841 he was working as a slater and plasterer and he and his wife, Ann who was born in Chippenham, Wiltshire, were living in Kineton Hills, Temple Guiting with two children, Agatha aged 2 and Emma who was baptised on 8 May 1841 in Temple Guiting. In 1844 they had another son, Thomas, who was baptised on 28 June and a further son, William, was baptised in Guiting Power on 11 April 1852.

By 1861 William Shepherd was a master slater and plasterer and his son, Thomas, was also working as a slater and plasterer. The family were living at 'Kennel', Guiting

Power. William's daughter, Agatha Shepherd, was working as a servant in the house of retired Lt Col Chisholm at 31 Clarence Square, Cheltenham and William's daughter, Emma, had also left home and was working as a house servant at Dymock Grange. Emma married William East in 1867. William East, who was born in Kineton, had started work as a plough boy aged 9, as did his elder brother, and by 1871 William and Emma were also living in Guiting Power where he was working as an agricultural labourer. William Shepherd's daughter, Agatha, married Levi Billington in 1862. They had a daughter, Alexandra Elizabeth, in 1863 in Cheltenham but Levi died in 1864. By 1871 Alexandra was living with her grandparents, William and Ann Shepherd, in Guiting Power, where William was still working as a plasterer. William and Emma East were still living in Guiting Power where they had two daughters, Margaret, born 1875 and Lily, baptised 1 March 1973. By 1881 William and Ann Shepherd were living in one of two cottages called Moor Cottages in Guiting Power. Their granddaughter, Alexandra Billington, who was working as a domestic servant was still living with them. William was still working as a plasterer. Alexandra's mother, Agatha, a widow, was living in Cheltenham at 9, Lower Park Street working as a needlewoman. In 1890 when she was 50 Agatha married Thomas Banks of Alderton who had been married twice before and had 8 children from those previous marriages. Thomas died in 1896.

Both William and Ann Shepherd lived to a good age. They entered Winchcombe workhouse together on 25 August 1905 when William was 91 and Ann was 95 and Ann died there in 1906. They would have had to live in segregated quarters in the workhouse. When William Shepherd was in Winchcombe workhouse he was visited by Sheila Rathbone on 1 January 1908 when he sang *Yonder Sits A Spanish Lady*. She said that he 'sang rather low but said his words very distinctly.' She wrote to Percy Grainger about her visit to the Workhouse the following day and Percy Grainger visited the Workhouse on 5 April 1908 when William 'Daddy' Shepherd aged 93 sang him courting songs *American Stranger, Brisk Sailor Lad, Green Bushes, Jolly Joe (The Collier's Son), Seeds of Love, The Young Fisherman, Yonder Sits A Spanish Lady and My Love's Gone,* the tales of *Bold General Wolfe* and *Saucy Jack Tar* and the *Shepherd's Song*. Cecil Sharp then visited him on 8 April 1909 and he then sang *Oh no John, Joe the Pen Collier, Who Knocks There* (recitation only), *We'll All Stand Up* and *The Bold Fisherman* (tune only known). William remained in the Workhouse and died there on 19 June 1909 shortly after being recorded by Percy Grainger.

As many people stayed in the same area for all of their lives and had large families there was often more than one person with the same name in an area. For example, there was another William Shepherd in Winchcombe workhouse at the same time as William 'Daddy' Shepherd, this time from the village of Alderton.

So it is not always easy to tell which person was the singer; for example there were also two Mr Tandys in Winchcombe workhouse at the same time. Percy Grainger visited **Mr Tandy**, a former labourer, in Winchcombe Workhouse on 5 April 1908 when he sang courting songs *The Farmer's Lad, The Irish Girl, Nancy, Susan And Her Lovers*, and *There Was an Old Man (Green Broom)*. There were two George Tandys in Winchcombe Workhouse around this time but one George Tandy from Guiting Power was discharged from the Workhouse the day before Grainger's visit on 5 April 1908 so George Tandy from Alderton must have been the person recorded by Grainger.

George Tandy was baptised on 17 October 1841 in Alderton, the son of George and Elizabeth Tandy. His father was a shoemaker and his mother, Elizabeth, was born in Charlton Cropthorne, Worcestershire. By 1851 his father had died but his mother was still living in Alderton with George's two elder sisters, Rosana born about 1828 and Harriett born about 1831, both of whom were working as glove makers, and three brothers, Caleb baptised 15 November 1835 (probably died in 1868), Edwin baptised 18 February 1838, (probably died in 1843), and Charles born about 1845. George also had two other sisters, Elizabeth born about 1826 and Helen/Ellen baptised 26 May 1833. All the children were born in Alderton and by 1851 George, Caleb, Edwin and Charles were all working as agricultural labourers. By 1861 George Tandy had left home and was one of two lodgers in Bye Street, Ledbury in the house of James Hodges, a carpenter. Both lodgers were working as excavators. George moved around for his work and by 1871 he was one of seven railway labourers living in the Roman Road railway huts, Appleby, Crackenthorpe, Westmoreland with George Thomas, another railway labourer, and his family. It is difficult to follow George Tandy's life after this date but there is a possible marriage of George Tandy to Fanny Stevens in Cheltenham on 26 December 1875 and the birth of a child, Albert T. Tandy to George and Fanny Tandy of Dumbleton on 14 January 1872 which may be related.

George Tandy was in Winchcombe Workhouse by 1906 and remained there until his death when he was buried in Winchcombe on 14 September 1918. Life was not always easy there as is shown by a record of the Master of the Workhouse which stated in March 1906: 'I also beg to report that on the 5th Instant inmates George Tandy No 2 and Edmund Skillern while employed digging in the garden quarrelled and that Tandy struck Skillern on the right eye (blind) which caused the eye to burst – this eye was taken out by Dr Cox at the Cottage Hospital on the 6th Instant and Tandy after being reprimanded twice was sentenced to 7 day imprisonment. I consider Skillern the aggressor.'

Another singer who was recorded by Percy Grainger in Winchcombe workhouse was **Mrs Elizabeth Teale**. Percy

Grainger visited Mrs Teale, aged over 60 from Bishop's Cleeve, at Winchcombe Workhouse on 24 August 1908 when she sang *Cold Blows The Wind* and *Lord Lovell*. He noted that she was *'60 years of age and rather gone in the head.'*

Elizabeth's husband, George Teale was born in Stow on the Wold in about 1842, the son of William Wood Teale, born in Lower Swell, who was the publican of the Plough Inn at Bishop's Cleeve in 1861 and his wife Ann who was born in Witcombe. By 1861 George Teale was working as an agricultural labourer. In 1871 George Hall Teale and his wife, Elizabeth, were living in Stoke Road, Bishop's Cleeve, where George was working as an agricultural labourer and Elizabeth was a laundress. George and Elizabeth were still living in Bishop's Cleeve in Evesham Road in 1891 where George was a market gardener. By 1901 they were living on Stoke Road, Bishop's Cleeve; George was then working as a general labourer. Mrs Elizabeth Teale was admitted to Winchcombe Workhouse on 7 December 1907 and then discharged on 18 May 1908. George Teale of Bishop's Cleeve was also admitted to the Workhouse late in 1907 and discharged on 13 January 1908. George Teale died and was buried in Bishop's Cleeve on 17 January 1908. Elizabeth Teale was admitted again to Winchcombe Workhouse on 27 November 1908 and discharged on12 November 1909 to be removed to the Asylum at Gloucester. Elizabeth Teale remained there until her death and she was buried in Bishop's Cleeve on 22 April 1910.

Another interesting singer from Winchcombe workhouse was **Archer Lane**, a former labourer, who sang *The Twelve Apostles* to Percy Grainger in Winchcombe Workhouse in 1908. Grainger stated that he was a native of Winchcombe.

Archer Lane was born in 1838 in Winchcombe, the son of James Lane, a labourer, and his wife Mary. In 1841 he was living with this parents in Castle Street, Winchcombe, together with his two brothers, Charles aged 11 and James aged 8 months and his three sisters, Hannah aged 9, Mary aged 7 and Eleanor aged 5. By 1851 the family had moved to Vineyard Street, Winchcombe and he and his father, mother and brothers, Charles and James, were all agricultural labourers. By then he also had another sister, Elizabeth, aged 7 and a brother, George, aged 4 both of whom were 'Sunday scholars', presumably only attending school on Sundays. Archer Lane enlisted in 4th Battalion of the Rifle Brigade in 1857 and had 16 years military service. He was a Private in the Rifle Brigade stationed at Chatham Barracks in the 1871 census. Percy Grainger stated that Archer Lane had been in Corfu, Malta, Gibraltar and Canada.

In 1878 he married Eliza Houlton who was born in Bolton, the daughter of a cotton weaver, and by 1891 was living with her at 3, Miner's Row in Pendleton in Salford in Lancashire. He was working as a general labourer and she was a cotton winder. They moved back to Winchcombe and Eliza died towards the end of 1901. Archer Lane was in Winchcombe workhouse at least from October 1899, described as an agricultural labourer. He remained there until at least February 1901, then was discharged from there before returning on 12 July 1901. He remained in the Workhouse until at least 20 February 1901 when the Workhouse Master reported that Archer Lane had been helping to nurse inmates with the disease erysipelas. He was back in the Workhouse from 2 January 1905 until 26 March 1905 and then back there again on 3 January 1906. Life was not always easy there as on 14 August 1909 the Master's report stated, *'I beg to report Edmund Skillern for fighting and striking inmate George Care across the face with a handsaw on the 5th Instant and also with quarrelling this morning with another inmate i.e. Archer Lane.'* However in 1911 he was given leave to attend a Veterans Dinner in Cheltenham on Empire Day 24 May 1911. Eleanor Adlard of Postlip Hall supervised the transport of the veterans to the dinner. *(Fig 47)*

Fig. 47.

Archer Lane remained in the workhouse until his death on 23 January 1912.

Another of the singers recorded by Percy Grainger in Winchcombe Workhouse was **Mr R. Wakefield** when he sang *The Constant Farmer's Son* on 5 April 1908.

Robert Wakefield was born in 1839 in Calmesden near North Cerney. He was the son of James Wakefield, a shepherd born in 1791 in North Cerney, the son of William and Esther Wakefield.

He was admitted to Winchcombe Workhouse on 13 April 1905 where he remained until 25 July 1905 but was discharged from there again on 25 July 1906. He was back in the workhouse by July 1907 where he remained until 3 February 1911 when he left the workhouse to move in with his daughter, Sarah Ann, and her family in Withington. Robert Wakefield died in 1918 in the Northleach registration district. For further details of his life see Chapter 2 Occupations above.

Sometimes in spite of having children, parents still ended up in the workhouse if the children were unable to look after them, for example when they did not earn very much. Such was probably the case with **'Richard Thomas Toms'** of Fairford aged 85 whom Cecil Sharp visited at Cirencester Union workhouse on 2 November 1911 when he sang the songs *Botany Bay* and *A Virgin Unspotted*. Cirencester Union comprised many parishes:-Ampney Crucis, Ampney St. Mary,

Ampney St. Peter, Badgington, Barnsley, Baunton, Brimpsfield, Cirencester, Coates, Colesborne, Daglingworth, Down Ampney, Driffield, Duntisbourne Abbots, Duntisbourne Rouse, Edgworth, Elkstone, Fairford, Harnhill, Hatherop, Kemble, Kempsford, Maisey Hampton, North Cerney, Poole Keynes, Poulton, Preston, Quenington, Rendcombe, Rodmarton, Sapperton, Shomcote, Siddington, Somerford Keynes, Syde, South Cerney, Stratton and Winstone. It was a stone building erected in 1836, for 330 inmates. But by 1891 the population of the union was 20,398; it covered area 86,183 acres and its rateable value in 1897 was £113,095.

'Richard Toms' was probably Richard Tombs, born in Kempsford and baptised there on 25 September 1825. He was the son of John Tombs, a labourer and his wife, Amy. In 1850 he married Elizabeth Evans in the Cirencester registration district and by 1861 they were living in East End, Fairford with three children, Eliza born about 1849 in Horcutt, John born about 1852 in Fairford and Caroline born about 1854 in Fairford. In 1871 they were still living at East End, Fairford. John was still living at home and they had another two children, Ann born about 1863 and Rose Ellen born about 1868 both born in Fairford. Richard and John were both working as labourers. In 1881 they were still living at East End, Fairford where Richard was working as a labourer and Rose Ellen was the only child still living at home. In 1891 Richard and Elizabeth were living at 9 London St., Fairford and at home with them was a grandchild, George Richard Lee, who had been born in London.

After the death of his wife, Richard Tombs, still described as an agricultural labourer, lived with his daughter Ann. She had married Albert Winstone, also an agricultural labourer, born in Quenington, had six children and lived in London Road, Fairford. Richard was living with them in 1901 until they moved to a farm in Aldsworth when we can speculate that none of his other children could look after him – Richard's daughter Eliza had married a coal miner, had eleven children and lived in the Rhondda Valley, and his daughter Rose Ellen had married a railway signalman, had two children and lived in Ledbury. By 1911 he had gone to the workhouse in Cirencester where he died in the infirmary in 1915.

(See also Chapter 1 Forest of Dean Musicians for Newent workhouse and the musician Stephen Baldwin.)

My Love's Gone

As I was a - - walk - ing down by the sea shore
Where the wind and the waves and the bill - - ows did roar,
Where the wind and the waves and the wa - - ters run down
I heard a shrill voice make a sor - - row - - ful sound,
Cry - - ing, "Oh my love's gone who I does a - - dore.
He's gone and I nev - er, no nev - er, shall see my love more."

2. "Oh why should I mourn for my true love who's slain
   While his body lies under the watery main?
   The shells of the oysters shall make my love's bed,
   And the shrimps of the sea shall swim over his head."
   Crying, "Oh my love's gone who I does adore.
   He's gone and I never, no never, shall see my love more."

3. As I was a-going to go on my way
   I heard this fair damsel so pleasant and gay.
   She'd thrown her fair body right into the deep
   And closed up her eyes in the water to sleep.
   Crying, "Oh my love's gone who I does adore.
   He's gone and I never, no never, shall see my love more"

Source: William Shepherd, aged 93, Winchcombe, 5th April 1908, collected by Percy Grainger

© Gloucestershire Traditions

The Sweet Briar

Source: John Mason, fiddle, at Stow-on-the-Wold, on 2 August 1909, coll. CJ Sharp no 2234
Notes: "Country Dance"

©Gloucestershire Traditions

4

GYPSY SINGERS

The term 'gypsy' can cover a number of different communities, from Irish tinkers to 'new age travellers' to the traditional gypsy. The history of gypsies is quite complex, but for the purposes of this book we are talking about the old-style English communities that would travel from place to place, living off their wits and off seasonal work. Gypsies have long been a part of the rural scene in Gloucestershire. The arterial roads that link up the south-west, the Midlands and Wales have seen many a gypsy caravan over the years and the fruit and vegetable growing areas of the Vale of Evesham and the hop-growing areas further north have been magnets for the travelling folk.

Today's gypsies lead a different life. The mechanisation of farming has been one of the factors that has changed their traditional way of life. Today's gypsies are less likely to be the travelling people but are rooted in their local area, involving themselves in trades such as scrap metal, tarmacking, tree surgery and so on – trades that require skill with their hands. The roadside gypsies are seldom seen except for occasions such as the twice-yearly Stow Fair and those gypsies who have not moved into houses generally live in organised sites.

By the same token, the traditions have been diluted. Most

of the old folk songs are not sung and it is rare to find gypsy musicians playing the old tunes or performing step dances, preferring instead songs of Americana. The singers and musicians described below were possibly some of the last of the old breed.

THE BRAZIL FAMILY

Gypsies have been one of the most prolific sources of traditional songs in Gloucestershire. Their oral traditions have kept alive many of the songs which would otherwise have been lost. One of the best families of singers and musicians in Gloucestershire were the Brazil family. *(Fig 48)* Parents William and Priscilla Brazil came from the West Country to live in London. We know that one of the older children, Lementina or

Fig. 48.

'Lemmie', was born near Southampton but the family then moved to Ireland where they travelled for around 27 years and where most of their children were born. They then returned to Gloucestershire in 1919. They had 15 children.

The Children: [22]
Bill (William) died: 1940.
Omie (Naomi) age 78 (Mrs Evans, Wales).
Lemmie (Lementina) born near Southampton age 77.
Tom (Thomas) died 1967 (Newent).
Beccy (Rebecca) (Mrs Thomas – wife of a Welsh collier).
Priscilla (Mrs Thomas – wife of a Welsh collier, brother of the above).

Hyram (Harold) age 76? Gloucester.

Daughter Joan Taylor.

Alice (Mrs Webb, Tewkesbury Common).

Son – name presently unknown to us.

Janey (Jane) (Mrs T Swan, Gloucester).

Florence (Mrs Bill Sparrow, Frampton).

Harry and wife Dolly born 1 March 1901 in Ireland, Gloucester.

Son Charlie, daughter Doris, married to Gilbert Davies, daughters Debbie and Pennie.

Danny and wife Betty born in Ireland, Gloucester.

Daughters Doris married to Riley Stephens, Alice married to Connor Smith. Son Billy in Ireland.

Pat born in Ireland.

Weenie (Selphinus) and wife Ethel. born in Ireland, travelled in Scotland, d: 1966 (Scotland).

Son Albert. Daughters Maudie, Angela, married to Jimmy Winston.

Peter born 1907 possibly in Ireland, age 61 living near Newent.

The last surviving member of this generation (as far as we know) was Danny, who died in September 2003.

Fig. 49. Danny Brazil
(Photo: Paul Burgess)

Many members of the Brazil family were singers or musicians. *(Fig 50)* The Scottish poet Hamish Henderson was the first person to record them when he met Weenie Brazil in Blairgowrie during the July/August berrypicking season of 1955. He recorded Weenie and his daughter, Angela, for the School of Scottish Studies. Peter Shepheard then made many recordings of the family in Gloucestershire from 1966 onwards and Gwilym Davies

Fig. 50.

and Rod Smith in 1977-78. Mike Yates in 1978 also recorded the family and Gwilym Davies went back to record them in the 1990s. Peter Shepheard put together a book of the family's songs from his recordings which he presented to the family.

The two members of the family with the widest range of songs were the brothers Harry and Danny Brazil. Peter Shepheard first met Harry's daughter, Doris, who married into another local traveller family, the Davieses. At the time she was living at a site in Eastington. Doris's daughters Pennie and Debbie were later recorded for Topic records. Harry Brazil had a good voice and was subsequently recorded. He married Doris Morgan in Gloucester in 1924. He lived in a trailer at Sandhurst near Gloucester and used to sing at the Pelican pub in Gloucester while the women went to play Bingo. He sang a wide range of songs including many songs about life in the country such as *The Poacher, If I were a Blackbird, A Blacksmith Courted Me* and *The Bold Keeper,* Irish songs such as *Sally Marone* and courting songs such as *The Gown So Green* and *The Loyal Lover.*

Harry's brother, Danny Brazil, also had a large repertoire of traditional songs and was a noted stepdancer, singer and mouth organ player. Unfortunately an altercation with Harry left him with an injured voice box which made singing difficult. However he had a tremendous memory for the words of songs and was able to convey the tune of many songs to the song collectors Peter Shepheard in the 1960s and Gwilym Davies and Mike Yates in the 1970s. Gwilym made further recordings of Danny in the 90s.

Danny Brazil lived in a trailer in Staverton Road, Churchdown. He had at least 50 songs in his huge repertoire covering many types of songs, from ballads to courting songs which he sang in the family and in pubs. Danny's recall of the words of his songs was remarkable and he would be reluctant to start a song unless he could sing it right through. He said that although many of his fellow gypsies were singing Country and Western songs, this was not a genre that interested him much and that he preferred to sing what he termed 'folk songs'. He was a driver in World War II and took part in the liberation of Berlin. By the 1990s he had moved to the traveller site in Elmstone Hardwicke near another good gypsy singer, Wiggy Smith, and the latter's respect for Danny, 20 years his senior, was evident.

In Danny's latter years he suffered bad health and had an operation to amputate a leg but his mind remained sharp. Danny Brazil died in Gloucester, in September 2003.

Danny's daughter Alice married Connor Smith, son of Biggun Smith and nephew of Denny Smith, both of whom were also singers. Danny's daughter, Doris, married Riley Stephens who was not himself a singer but was keen for Peter Shepheard to meet his grandfather, and travelled with him to Bristol in May 1966 to meet both his grandfather Tom (Chappie) Stephens and uncle Mark Stephens (d.1973), from both of whom he recorded songs.

Harry and Danny's elder sister, Lemmie (Lementina) was a singer and melodeon player. In her younger days she had also played fiddle and mouth organ. When younger in Ireland she said that she would sing at the crossroad and when she had finished raise her skirt to collect money in it. She lived in the same traveller site as Harry in Sandhurst, Churchdown, in a trailer with no electricity, She had a similar repertoire of songs to her brothers but also some unusual songs which the others in the family didn't sing such as *The Irish Girl,* the *Bonny Black Hare* and *Little Sir Hugh*. She also had a large repertoire of dance tunes which she played on her Hohner one-row melodeon, including hornpipes and step dance tunes.

Fig. 51. Lemmie Brazil (photo: Mike Yates)

Another brother, Hyram Brazil was also a singer as was Hyram's daughter, Joan Brazil.

JOAN TAYLOR

Fig. 52. Joan Taylor

Fig. 53.

Joan was one of 5 children and was born in 1931 in Swindon but did not know whether she was born in a hospital or in the family caravan. *(Fig 53)*

She lived her early years on the road, based in Gloucester, where the family wintered, travelling around in the summer for seasonal work around Evesham including fruit and hop picking and driving a threshing machine, and hawking flowers, pegs and rush mats from door to door – "All honest hard work".

She recalled her family singing and although could not sing any of her father's songs, she picked up songs from other family members and friends. She remembered her uncles step dancing, Harry 'diddling' for Danny and vice versa. Her splendid singing is very much in gypsy style, with attention to phrasing and the tone of the voice.

In 1968, she and her husband Charlie Taylor and three children moved into a house in Quedgeley, Gloucester, and established a business selling coal and hiring out skips, despite neither being able to read or write. When she died in Gloucester in 2016, she had 5 children, a number of grandchildren and even a great-great (sic) grandchild. A recording taken by Gwilym Davies of her singing *"Can I Sleep in your Barn Tonight, Mister"* was played at her funeral service.

WIGGY SMITH

Wiggy was one of the last of the English traveller singers to sing old songs in the old style. He was born in a covered wagon near Bristol in the days when roadside gypsies were a more common sight than nowadays. His family travelled around the West Midland area in a horse-drawn trailer and knew true poverty of kind which is rare today. He and his family ended up in Gloucestershire where he lived until his death, although he always claimed that his roots were in Hampshire. The many skills he learnt in his lifetime included how to converse in Romany, how to fit a wheel on a wagon, how to go ferreting for

Fig. 54.
Wiggy Smith

rabbits and how to find the best edible mushrooms. At one time he earned a living as a prize fighter and remained fit and strong into his seventies. He spent his life living on his wits to provide for his wife Myra and large family. As Wiggy himself said *"The money wasn't about, but it was better times all round."* His descendants amounted to over 100 at his death, including great-grandchildren, all of whom he adored with fierce pride.

His songs were mainly learnt in the traditional way, from friends and family around the camp fire, or in the many pub sessions that accompanied fruit and vegetable picking in the area. However, he did learn a number of songs from a set of Jimmy Rodgers recordings which he prized.

Wiggy and his family were 'discovered' by the Cheltenham folk club scene in the early 1970s, by clubs singers including Ken Langsbury and Bernie Cherry, and before long his songs were being heard in the local folk clubs. This led to an invitation to Mike Yates to come and record the family in 1974 and to the release of a number of songs on Topic Records, namely *I took my dog, The Oakham Poachers* and *The Deserter* sung by Wiggy and *The Gallaway Man* and *Go from my Window* sung by Wiggy's father, also called Wisdom. Despite these recordings, Wiggy disappeared from view so far as the folk scene was concerned for about 20 years until a chance discussion between the seasoned song collectors Peter Shepheard and Gwilym Davies led to a visit to Wiggy in 1994. By this time he was living in a trailer on the modest Cursey Lane caravan park in Elmstone Hardwicke, Tewkesbury. At that first visit, he was helpful and friendly and sang them several snatches from his repertoire.

With the help of musicians from the Cheltenham Folk Song Club, some sessions were set up in the Victoria Public House, Wiggy's local in the run-down St Pauls area of Cheltenham. This led in turn to his being invited to a number of English Country Music Weekends at Postlip Hall, near Cheltenham. This was Wiggy's first encounter with the folk revival and he took to it immediately. The power and timing of his singing was compelling and a lesson to many there. The fact that he brought an unpredictability and spontaneity to the proceedings was brought home when on one occasion, on sitting through a performance of the *Holy Well* by a certain floor singer, he became increasingly restless, until at last he could contain himself no longer and called out in mid-verse *'Stop. It doesn't go like that.'* Imagine the singer's surprise when Wiggy then proceeded to sing his version of the same song, to the delight of the audience. Only Wiggy could have got away with it.

In the late 90s, Paul Burgess and Gwilym Davies spent many hours in Wiggy's company, playing music, singing songs and chatting. It was more than mere collecting songs. It was sharing his life reminiscences with him.

Wiggy's repertoire included folk songs, modern sentimental songs, George Formby songs, Irish songs, cowboy songs and snatches of step dances tunes. His favourite song was in fact *'You're the only good thing to have happened to me'* which he sang in memory of his late wife Myra. His singing is an object lesson to singers in the folk scene. His voice was strong and ringing and he never hurried a song. He had a way of drawing the listener into the song, even when he did not have the complete song, such as *Barbary Allen* of which he only knew 3 verses, but sang them in such a way that you felt you were hearing the complete story. It is probably not exaggerating to say that his hard life was reflected in his tough, no nonsense style of singing.

His last years were characterised by ill health, but he was nursed tirelessly by his daughter Alice. When he passed away in 2002, 700 people attended the funeral at Cheltenham cemetery, of whom all but 4 were travellers. Six flat bed trucks were needed to take the flowers to Cheltenham Crematorium and a wake was held in the Hop Pole Inn in Gloucester Road, Cheltenham. As the grief subsided in the pub afterwards, the songs started to flow, including his version of '*The Deserter*', which could almost be seen as his epitaph:

> *I was once young and foolish like many who is here*
> *I've been fond of night rambling and I am fond of my beer*
> *But if I had my own home and my sweet liberty*
> *I would do no more soldiering by land or by sea.*

MR FLETCHER AND ISOBEL FLETCHER

We know that other gypsies sang traditional songs in Gloucestershire but because of their itinerant lifestyle it is sometimes hard to glean information about them. An example of this is the Fletchers. Cecil Sharp visited Mr Fletcher in Cinderford on 5 September 1919 when he noted the words for the extremely rare ballad, *The Wife of Usher's Well*, plus a fragmentary version of *King Herod and the Cock*. Two weeks later, Sharp visited the Fletchers again and noted the words of *The Crafty Maid's Policy* or *I Met a Fair Damsel* and *The Holy Well* from Isabel Fletcher, presumably Mr Fletcher's wife. Unfortunately, Sharp did not recover any tunes from the Fletchers, which suggests that they merely recited the songs to him.

Although there were several families with the name Fletcher living in Cinderford at the time of the 1901 census no Isabel Fletcher was noted. Neither was there any Isabel

Fletcher in the 1911 census in Cinderford. In a Durham University thesis in 1980 by Mary Diane McCabe entitled 'A critical study of some traditional religious ballads', she states that these songs were sung by 'Mrs. Isabel Fletcher, a gypsy, in 1919'. So if Isabel Fletcher was a gypsy that would explain why she does not feature in the census returns.

KATHLEEN WILLIAMS

Another Gloucestershire gypsy singer was Kathleen Williams who was visited by Cecil Sharp at Wigpool Common, Mitcheldean on 6 September 1921. She knew a variety of traditional songs including ballads and courting songs and sang him *Barbara Ellen, Bessie Watson or The Brisk Young Lover, Green Mossy Banks of the Lea, The Indian Lass, Jock of Hazeldean, Saddle My Horse, T for Thomas* and *When First to This Country a Stranger*.

We do not have any more information about her family but Sharp saw her again at Puddlebrook near Drybrook on 9 September when she sang him *The Crab Fish* and *The Little Girl* and also *The Fat Buck* or *Thorneymoor Woods, The One Cow* and *Still Growing* and he saw her again at Drybrook on 11 September 1921 when she sang him *The Cuckoo, I'm 17 Come Sunday, The Unquiet Grave* and *The White Cockade*.

Sharp commented '*Mrs Williams is a gypsy – about 60 or more – living in a van on the edge of a hill covered in heathers and gorse by the roadside, living with her married son and his three children, Henry, Dolly and Rosie.*' Nothing more is known about Mrs Williams but the name Kathleen suggests an Irish background. Interestingly, many of her songs were still being sung in Gloucestershire by the Brazil family up to the 1970s.

The Bold Keeper

1. It's of a bold kee-per in the chase of his deer, He cour-ted a
no-ble-man's daugh-ter so fair. If you are as wil-ling to
those church we'll ride, And there you'll get mar-ried brave la-dy of mine.

2. As they were riding through meadows so wide
   With a broad sword and buckle hung down by his side,
   There he met her father and twenty brave men,
   With a broad glittering sword drawn ready in hands.

3. "Now it's bold keeper, don't you stand to prattle,
   I can see by the movements they means for a battle."
   They cut and they slain till the ground they stood on,
   And the lady held the horse for bold keeper.

4. "Now it's bold keeper, come pray hold my hands
   You shall have my daughter, ten thousands in hand."
   (repeat tune of lines 1-2)
   "Oh no, dearest father, it's too small of sum."
   "You'll hold your tongue daughter, your will shall be done.
   If you are as willing to those church you'll ride
   And there you'll get married, brave lady of mine."

Source: Sung by Harry Brazil, Sandhurst Gloucester. Collected by Gwilym Davies 18/02/1978.

The Fat Buck
(In Thorney Moor Woods)

In Thun-der-man-shire there was a fat buck, Right fol de dol a ear I day, In
Thun-der-man-shire there was a fat buck, Right fol de dol ear I day. The
ve-ry first night we did go out, Oh one of our best dogs he got shot And
he was the best dog out of the lot, Right fol de dol ear I day.

Alternative

2. For he came to me both bloody and lame,
   And sorry was I for to see the same,
   I said he weren't able to follow the game,
   Right fol the dol ear I day.
   Then if this is hunting I'll give o'er
   And hunting I shall go no more
   For to catch a fat buck in Thundermanshire,
   Right fol the dol ear I day.

3. If you ever saw poor limping Jack
   A-carrying the first quarter all on his back,
   He carried it like some beggarman's sack,
   Right fol the dol ear I day.
   Then if this be hunting, etc.

4. Now the very first quarter we had over for sale
   It was to an old woman who sold bad ale.
   She was the cause of us poor lads to go to gaol
   Right fol the dol ear I day.
   Then if this be hunting, etc.

5. Now our 'sizes thay are drawing near
   And we are all quaking for fear
   All through this old woman who sold bad beer.
   Right fol the dol ear I day.
   Then if this be hunting, etc.

Source: Collected by Cecil Sharp from Mrs Kathleen Williams, Puddlebrook nr Drybrook,
September 9, 1921

5

WOMEN SINGERS AND MUSICIANS

What sort of songs did the women sing?

Farm labourers' wives had a hard life. As well as working alongside their men in the fields they were expected to raise large families to bring in income and fight the high death rate of children, for example, one singer, Mrs Wiggett of Ford, was one of at least nine children. Many of their songs were about courting and young love. They also knew some of the old ballads, for example tales about Robin Hood and were a good source for local versions of Christmas carols and hymns. The women also retained children's songs sung in their childhood.

In the past many young girls **went into service** but it seems to be mainly the men who sang songs about the experiences of servant girls. Many others worked as **glovers**, making gloves at home by hand stitching.

This chapter looks at some of the more important women traditional singers and musicians that we know of in Gloucestershire.

EMILY BISHOP

One of the more important traditional women singers was

Emily Bishop who, with her sister Beatrice, was visited by the song collector, Russell Wortley, in 1956/7 at Bromsberrow Heath, a village in Gloucestershire but with an address outside the County because of the location of the nearest Postal Sorting Office. Her father, who came originally from Gloucester, kept the Bell public house in Bromsberrow Heath and was the Morris "King". The song collector, Peter Kennedy, also recorded Emily Bishop.

Fig. 55. Russell Wortley collecting from Beatrice Hill and Emily Bishop.
Photo: Cambridge Morris Archive

Emily Bishop was a fine singer and had a large repertoire of songs:

- songs of young love and courting such as *Barbary Allen, Banks of Sweet Primroses, Dark Eyed Sailor, If I'm Dirty Love, Just as the Tide was Flowing, Clear Away the Morning Dew, No Sir No, Raggle Taggle Gypsies-O* and *Seventeen Come Sunday*
- Christmas and religious songs such as *Catch the Sunshine, Christmas Is Now Drawing Near At Hand, , Dives and Lazarus, The Little Room, The Angel Gabriel, A Fountain of Christ's Blood, The Line To Heaven, On Christmas Night All Christians Sing, The Moon Shines Bright* and *A Virgin Unspotted*
- Ballads such as *Lord Lovel*

- Songs of life in the countryside such as the *Northamptonshire Poacher* and *Wassail Song*,
- Music hall songs such as *Riding in the Railway Train*

Beatrice and Emily's grandfather, Thomas Bishop, was born in Leigh, Worcestershire in 1799. He married Mary Reynolds from Taynton, Gloucestershire, in 1847 in the Newent registration district and by 1851 he was described in the Census as a' labourer pauper' living in Ryton, Dymock Ryland, with their son, Thomas, born in 1848, Beatrice and Emily's father. Also living with them were Joseph and Edwin 'Randals' aged 11 and 8 – probably 'Reynolds' from a previous marriage of Mary's. By 1861 they were still living in the same village where Thomas was an agricultural labourer. They had two further children living at home, Mary Ann, born about 1853, and James, born about 1855, both born in Dymock. Thomas died in 1863 in the Gloucester registration district.

By 1861 their son, Thomas, had left home and was living in Ketford, Dymock Ryland, as a servant and agricultural labourer in the house of James Young, a farm bailiff. In 1869 he married Fanny Poole from Chosen (Hill), Gloucester, in the Newent registration district. Fanny already had at least one daughter, Ellen, born 1868, and by 1871 they were living in Bromsberrow Heath with two children, Mary A. born about 1867 and Ellen born 1868. Living in the same house were Mary, Thomas' mother and his siblings Mary A. a 'late housemaid' and James, an agricultural labourer.

Fig. 56. Probably Thomas and Fanny Bishop

Emily was born to Thomas and Fanny in early 1879 in Bromsberrow Heath but by 1881 the family had moved to Ryton, Dymock with further children, Annie born about 1871, Henry born about 1873, Alan born about 1878 and Alice born about 1879. Thomas' mother, Mary, was still living with them, working as a laundress, as was Thomas' stepdaughter, Ellen Pool(e). Beatrice Fanny Bishop was born in 1881 but her mother, Fanny, died in 1884. Thomas remarried in 1885, to Mary Gittings, who already had at least one son, Thomas A. Gittings, born in Ledbury, Herefordshire about 1881. Thomas Gittings is believed to have emigrated to the USA and was buried in the Lloyd Cemetery in Ebensburg, Cambria County, Pennsylvania in 1952.Thomas Bishop continued to live in Ryton with his new wife, Mary and by 1891 they were living there with his children, Alice L., Emily and Beatrice, and her daughter, Mary Gittings. Thomas' wife, Mary, died in 1893 and by 1901 he was still living in a cottage in Ryton with his daughters Anne, a housemaid (domestic) and Alice L. He was still there in 1911 with his daughters, Annie who was a housekeeper and Emily who had moved back home and was a housemaid.

Fig. 57. Emily Bishop, early 1900s

Emily Bishop had left home by 1901 when she was probably working as a housemaid at the Nordrach-sur-Mendip

TB Hospital in Somerset. By 1911 she had moved back home with her father in Ryton and was working as a housemaid. She never married and died in 1961 in Bromsberrow Heath, now in Herefordshire.

Beatrice and Emily's brother, Alan Bishop, in the 1891 census was living in Gloucester and in 1901 was working for the Metropolitan police in London. In the photograph, which was probably taken in the late 1890s, Police Constable Bishop's collar number is 505 'B' which would indicate he would have been patrolling the Chelsea District of London and could have been attached to either Gerald Road, Kensington or Walton Street Police stations. The armband denotes that the officer is 'on duty'.

In the 1911 census he was living in Canada and fought with a Canadian Regiment in the Great War.

Fig. 58. Alan Bishop early 1900s

Beatrice and Emily's sister, Annie, had left home by 1891 and was working at Longford Park in 1901. The same year she moved back home to live with her father, Thomas Bishop and was still there in 1911.[23]

Fig. 59. Annie Bishop at Longford Park in 1901

MARY ANN CLAYTON

Mary Ann Clayton was one of the most important folk song sources in Gloucestershire, particularly for the carol *The Holly and The Ivy,* Gloucestershire's most famous folksong export to the world, of which Mary sang 3 verses and the tune to Cecil Sharp. This is the version which was published and now has become the standard carol which is sung at Christmas. Mary was born circa 1846, probably in Alderton, Worcestershire. Little is known of her early life but she bore a daughter, Elizabeth, in about 1882 when she was living in Campden. By the time she met Sharp she was a widow, still living in the same house in Sheep Street, Chipping Campden. She may have been married to a Thomas Clayton who was living in Sheep Street in 1871 and had three daughters and two sons with his wife, Mary Ann, but it also possible that this is just a coincidence of name. Local tradition says that Mary Clayton, though not a Campden resident in her youth, was a then a visitor to the vicarage and only came to live here in the very early C20. She may have been a tenant of the Thatched Cottage. Thus there are some ambiguities concerning Mary but we have a lasting legacy of her songs.

ELIZABETH SMITHERD (NÉE HAYNES)

Elizabeth Smitherd had a large repertoire of songs. Cecil Sharp visited her in Tewkesbury on 9-10 January and 10-11 April 1908. She knew various songs of young love such as *A Brisk Young Man, As Jockey on a Summer's Morn, Blow Away the Morning Dew, The Cuckoo, Green Mossy Banks of the Lea, In Shepherd Park, It's of a Young Damsel, Jack Williams, The Miser's Daughter, My Bonny Bonny Boy, O Once I Courted a Fair Pretty Maid* and *Still Growing*, and songs of the army and the sea such as *The Orange and Blue, The Cruel Ship's Carpenter, Our Captain Called All Hands* and *A Sailor and Beautiful Wife*. She also knew the ballad the *Unquiet Grave* and the country song, the *Poaching Song*.

Elizabeth Haynes was born in Pamington in 1846 and baptised in the Parish Church at Ashchurch on 3 July 1853. She was the daughter of Ann and Thomas (also known as John) Haynes who was a carpenter and said to be a squire's son. She was one of thirteen sisters and learned all her folk songs from them and her parents. Elizabeth does not appear in the 1861 Census when she would have been 15, by which time her father, then a widower, had moved back to his birthplace of Aston on Carrant with only two of his daughters, Rose and Sarah. In the following Census of 1871 Elizabeth is found living on the Tewkesbury Road in Longford with Joseph Smitherd (also spelt Smilhards, Smithard, Smithered and Smithers), a tailor who gave his birthplace as London. Joseph had arrived in the Tewkesbury area after the death of his first wife, Sarah Ann Smitherd (née Witts), following the birth of their son, Herbert Samuel Smitherd, on the 10th November 1868, both events being registered at St George's, Hanover Square, London. Sadly, on the 5th January 1869 Herbert died of tuberculosis at Pamington, the death being registered at Tewkesbury by Joseph who was then living at

Kinsham near Bredon. It was presumably after these tragic losses that Elizabeth Haynes and Joseph Smitherd first met and went to live in Longford. Whilst they both recorded their surname as Smitherd, they do not appear to have married until the second quarter of 1875 when their marriage was registered at Cheltenham.

By 1881 they were living at 5 Station Street in Tewkesbury when Joseph gave his occupation as both Chelsea Pensioner and ironmonger's porter and his birthplace as Derby. However in subsequent Census returns he gave his occupation as general labourer and then timekeeper at the engineering works, and his birthplace as Derby and then Marylebone in London. Although Elizabeth did not have any children of her own she at times provided a home for her niece and nephew, Amy and Joseph Artus. She spent her final years at Barnes Almshouses (now demolished) in Spring Gardens off Chance Street, where she was described as the widow of Joseph Smitherd, an army pensioner. Elizabeth Smitherd died on 27 January 1910, only two years after Cecil Sharp's visit to Tewkesbury, and like her husband, Joseph, was buried in the town cemetery on the Gloucester Road.[24]

MRS WIGGETT

One singer who knew many songs about courting and young love was Mrs P. Wiggett who was visited by the song collector Cecil Sharp at the village of Ford on 9 April and 13 August 1909 (on his August visit Sharp spelled her name as Wickett). On this theme she sang him *The Shepherdess, The Broken Token, Riley, Blow The Fire Blacksmith, Young Banker* and *Jimmy and Nancy*.

Mrs Wiggett's maiden name was Lavinia Wearing and she was from a family of farm labourers, including her father,

Richard Wearing, and her grandfather, John Wearing. Her ancestors lived in Bledington at least back to 1760, including her great-great grandparents, John and Martha Wearing, her great-grandparents, Thomas and Elizabeth Wearing, her grandparents, John and Elizabeth Wearing and her parents Richard and Ann Wearing. Her grandfather was still living in Bledington in 1841. Her mother was from Upper Swell. Lavinia Wearing came from a large family and had at least three brothers and five sisters. Lavinia lived at home in Lower Swell with her parents until at least 1851.

In 1861 she married Percy Wiggett, an agricultural labourer born in 1840, but before this in about 1857 she had a son, William George, who in later life used the surname Warren. In the 1901 and 1911 Censuses it was stated that a Jabez Warren, a widower living with her, was her brother and William's uncle, so it would appear that William's father had the surname Warren. In 1861 Lavinia and Percy were living in Ford, next door to Percy's parents, with Lavinia's son, William George, who was using the surname Wiggett. By 1871 they had three daughters. A son, Percy, was born in 1881 but died at the age of 5. In 1891 the family were still living in the village of Ford where Percy had been working as a road contractor and labourer, and had two further daughters and a son, all born in Ford.

Lavinia's husband, Percy, died in 1897 and by 1901 Lavinia was still living in Ford, described as a retired farmer. A widow, she was living with her son, William George, who was then using the surname Warren and was a farmer employer. Also living in the same house were Jabez Warren, then described as her brother, a widower and carter on a farm, a nephew and a servant. Lavinia was living in a house next door to the Plough Inn which was then being kept possibly by Percy's brother Jesse. By 1911 William George Warren was head of the household and a farmer in Ford, still single. Living with him were Lavinia, aged

70, Jabez Warren, now described as his uncle, a widower and farm labourer, and a servant, Isaac Miles, a waggoner on farm. Jabez died in 1911 and Lavinia in 1916 aged 76.

MRS WIGGETT'S CHILDREN

As well as **William George Warren** (see above) Lavinia Wiggett had six daughters and two sons.

Lavinia's daughter, Ann Margret Wiggett was born in Harford Hill, Gloucestershire about 1862.

Lavinia's daughter, Elizabeth Wiggett was born about 1864 in Cutsdean. She worked as a domestic servant in the house of the High Street grocer, draper and postmaster in Bourton on the Water until her marriage to Raymond Fry from Greet who worked in a jam and sweet factory. She had a daughter who was a domestic maid.

Lavinia's daughter, Miriam Wiggett was born in Ford in 1867. She married Charles Humphries, a general labourer from Somerset, and they moved to Somerset where Charles worked as a railway labourer and then a timber feller and had ten children.

Miriam's son, Percy Samuel was a driver with the Royal Engineers during World War I and later in World War II joined the Home Guard.

Figs. 60 and 61.
Percy Wiggett

He died 27 August 2006. He had married Isobella Bishop in June 1914 in Bridgwater, Somerset and they probably had six daughters and a son.

Percy's daughter, Mabel Olive Humphries *(Fig 62)* married twice. She had two sons and a daughter from her first marriage and two sons from her second marriage. She died in 1998 in Westbury, Wiltshire. She firstly married John Ratcliffe Holland in Alton, Hampshire on 14 July 1951. He was born in Philadelphia on 12 November 1923 and had been previously married. He had his own firm in Shepton Mallet – J.R.Holland &Sons. They had four children and he died in Shepton Mallet on 8 October 1998.

Fig. 62.

Fig. 63. Mabel Olive Humphries and the Queen Mother

Fig. 64. John Ratcliffe Holland

Lavinia's daughter, Lucy Wiggett was born about 1869 in Ford and christened in Temple Guiting on 2 May 1869. No more is known about her.

Lavinia's daughter, Virginia Wiggett was born in Ford in 1872. She married George Troughton in 1890 in the Winchcombe registration district. By 1911 the family had moved to 13, School Road, Bengeworth, Evesham where George and his eldest son, Percy were both labourers at the jam works. They were probably employed at Messrs T.W. Beach and Sons Ltd factory as was Raymond Fry above. They had four sons.

Lavinia's son, Albert Allen Wiggett was baptised in Temple Guiting on 6 Jul 1879. He married Kate Caroline Bedford, who was born in Berkhamstead, Hertfordshire, in Brentford, Middlesex in 1899 they moved to Acton, Middlesex where Albert worked as a jobbing gardener. They had five children.

Their son, Leslie Allen Wiggett had married Winifred E. Gilling in Hammersmith in 1932 and between 1936 and 1964 they lived at 23 Shelley Avenue, Ealing. They had a son, Alan C. Wiggett, who was living with them at this address from 1959 to 1965. Leslie died on 9 February 1965 and was cremated in Breakspear Crematorium, Ruislip. His son, Alan C. Wiggett, married Helen J. Corrigham in Ealing in 1969.

Lavinia's son, Percy Wiggett was born in Ford in 1881 and baptised in Temple Guiting Church on 12 June 1881. He died aged 5 and was buried in Temple Guiting on 2 December 1886.

Lavinia's daughter, Florence Wiggett was born in Ford in 1887 and baptised in Temple Guiting Church on 1 April 1887. She married Robert Flower, a smallholder from Yorkshire. They had one daughter born about 1908 in Twyning.[25]

Mrs Cook

H. E. D. Hammond visited Mrs Cook aged 86 in Quedgeley about 1908 when she sang him *Robin Hood And The Widow's Three Sons*, one of many songs about good deeds by Robin Hood. He noted the words but not the tune.

Mrs Cook was probably born Aquila Speck in Hardwicke about 1824. She married Charles Cooke, a carpenter's son from Standish, in Haresfield on 12 April 1846. Their surname was variously spelled Cook or Cooke and her name as Aquila, Acquella or Aquella. Their daughter, Rhoda Cooke, was baptised on 21 Jun 1846 in Hardwicke and by 1851 they were living in Quedgeley where Charles was working as an agricultural labourer. By then they also had a son, also called Charles, born in Hardwick about 1848, who died at a young age and was buried in Quedgeley on 24 March 1853. Another son, Thomas, was baptised in Quedgeley on 4 December 1853 and by 1861 the family were living in Bristol Lane, Quedgeley, where Charles continued to work as an agricultural labourer. They also had two lodgers. Aquila and Charles Cooke then had another son, whom they also named Charles, who was baptised in Quedgeley in October 1861. Mrs Cooke's daughter, Rhoda Cooke, married Charles Chaplin, a farmer from Quedgeley, at the end of 1870 in Cheltenham. Rhoda had a son, also called Charles, in 1871 but by the time of the 1871 census her husband, Charles, had died and Rhoda was living at home with her parents at 4 Schoolhouse Cottages, Quedgeley.

By 1881 Charles Cooke, in addition to his agricultural work, had become Parish Clerk at St James' Church, Quedgeley. He and Aquila were living 'near the schoolhouse' in Quedgeley. Their son, Thomas, was working as a farm labourer and their other son, Charles, was working as a railway engine cleaner.

Fig. 65. Quedgeley Church

By 1891 Charles Cook had become church sexton in Quedgeley, in addition to working as a gardener, living in Church Lane, next door to the schoolmaster. His sons were then both agricultural labourers. In 1901 Charles and Aquila were still in Quedgeley where Charles Cooke was church clerk and his sons, Thomas and Charles, were working as a road labourer and a railway yard worker, both unmarried. Charles Cooke died and was buried in Quedgeley on 10 September 1904. Aquila continued to live in Quedgeley and was living there with her son, Charles, who was working as a general labourer in 1911. Aquila Cooke died and was buried in Quedgeley on 3 February 1915.

KEZIAH HAWKINS

Keziah Hawkins was visited by Cecil Sharp on 2 April 1907 in Old Sodbury when she gave him the words to the song, *The Twelve Joys of Mary*, a life of Christ from Mary's point of view. Her name, possibly derived from Hezekiah, was variously spelled Keziah, Kezzerah, Kessie and Heyiah Hawkins. The following day, Sharp obtained the tune for the song from Joseph Evans of Old Sodbury.

Keziah Hawkins was born prob. 1815-17 but the first record of her is in 1841 when, aged 25, she was married and living near Springsgrove Cottage, Old Sodbury, the wife of James Hawkins aged 25, a labourer. Her husband, James Hawkins, was born 31 July 1814 and a James Hawkins' burial was noted at Old Sodbury on 8 April 1881. His family came from Horton and his parents, John and Maria, had three other sons: William, George and Thomas and two daughters, Elizabeth, Eliza and Mary Ann born between 1814 and 1824. Kezia and James had nine children born between 1838 and 1858: William, John, Elizabeth, Edward, Mary Ann, Sara(h) Ann, Eileen, Ruth and Thomas. Her husband and all her children were born in Old Sodbury and were mainly agricultural labourers and lived in the areas of Mount Pleasant and the London and Bristol Road in Old Sodbury.

By 1871 her daughter, Ruth, was described an unemployed general servant living at home. In 1881 probably her son, Thomas Hawkins aged 23, an agricultural labourer was married and living on The Green, Old Sodbury with his wife, Caroline aged 21 and their son, William James, aged 7 months. Thomas had at least one other child, a daughter, Elizabeth, baptised in 1891.

As a widow in 1881 Keziah was described as a 'helper in garden' living by herself in Cotswold Lane, Old Sodbury and by 1891 she was aged 71 and living on Old Sodbury Hill with 'own means'. With her was her granddaughter, Elizabeth Hawkins, aged 5 who was born in Old Sodbury. By this time her son, Edward, was married to Harriet Drew and they were living in Old Road, Old Sodbury with their 4 children: James aged 15, Jesse aged 13, both agricultural labourers, and Ada aged 10 and Fred aged 5, both scholars.

By 1901 at age 84 she was 'unable to work on account of age' and living in' Froom Bridge', Old Sodbury with her son, Edward Hawkins, aged 55, now a farmer, his wife, Harriet aged 56, with their three children: Jesse, aged 23, a farmer's son, Ada, aged 20, a mother's help and Fred aged 15, a farmer's son, all born in Old Sodbury. They also had a boarder, Charles Petch, a railway Inspector born in Paddington. Edward and Harriet had nine children born between 1866 and 1886: Selina Mary (died aged 6), William Henry, Alice, Louise, James, Adam, Jesse, Ada and Fred. Edward died before 1911 but Keziah, now aged 94, continued to live with his widow, Harriet, in Frome Bridge, Old Sodbury. Harriet's son Fred aged 25, single, a carter on a farm, was also living with them.

Keziah Hawkins died aged 98 and was buried on 7 April 1915 in Old Sodbury

Edward and Harriet's son, Jesse, became a cowman and in the 1911 Census was living in Lyr Poor (poss Lye Grove), Badminton Road, Old Sodbury aged 33 with his wife Florence, Lucy aged 35 and 7 children aged between 7 years and 3 weeks: Edward ' Jhon' [sic] , Ernest Jesse, Florence Alice, Gladys, Ada, Dorothy Mary and a baby.The wife was born in Wiveliscombe, the baby in Lye Grove, and the rest of the family in Old Sodbury.

JESSIE HOWMAN

Miss Jessie Howman was the daughter of a builder and decorator in Stow on the Wold. Roy Palmer visited Miss Jessie Howman aged 72 at Stow on the Wold on 11 August 1966 when she sang him the childrens' songs: *The Farmer's in the Dell, May Garlands, Poor Sally sits a-weeping, See the Robbers Coming Through*, the probably music hall dialect song *Somersetshire*, a probable broadside song, *A Young Farmer's Son* and the more generally known songs, *There was a Jolly Miller* and *We Wish You a Merry Christmas*.

Gertrude Jessie Howman was born 6 April 1894 in Stow On The Wold, Gloucestershire, In 1901 she was living in Stow on the Wold with her parents, William Cox Howman aged 36, an employed builder and contractor and Esther May Howman aged 35 and her three sisters: Dorothy Esther Howman aged 11, Margaret Lucy Howman aged 10. Also living with them was Beatrice Emily Clarke aged 17, a general servant domestic. Esther was born in Oxford but the rest of the family were born in Stow on the Wold.

In 1911 Jessie was the head of a household of 2 males and 5 females in a private house in Sheep Street, Stow on the Wold. C. Howman (probably Jessie's aunt Caroline, William's eldest sister) was head of a household of 2 females in a 'house shop' in Church Street, Stow on the Wold.

Her father William Cox Howman was born on 6 September1864 in the regstration district of Stow On The Wold. In 1871 William aged 6 was living in Sheep Street, Stow with his parents, George Howman aged 40 a Master builder (junior partner) and Elizabeth Howman aged 45 and his five sisters: Helen Howman aged 13, Miriam Howman aged 11, Elizabeth Howman aged 9, Emily Howman aged 5, Susan Howman aged 2. George was born in Salperton and the rest of the family in Stow.

By 1881 William Howman was an apprentice aged 16 still living with his parents, George Howman, a builder aged 50 and Elizabeth Howman aged 54, and his four sisters: Caroline Howman aged 26, Fanny Howman aged 24, Emily Howman aged 15 and Susan Howman aged 12 a scholar. Elizabeth was born in Salperton and the rest of the family were born in Stow.

William Cox Howman married Esther May Alden in 1888 in the registration district of Oxford, Esther's birthplace and then by 1891 they were living in Stow on the Wold. He was 26 and working as a builder and they had two children: Dorothy E. Howman aged 1 and unnamed daughter Howman aged 3 weeks. Also living with them was Ruth Arthurs aged 14, a general servant. William and the children were born in Stow. William C. Howman died 11th

September 1944 aged 80 in the North Cotswold registration district, Gloucestershire.

In the 1925 phone book the firm of William Cox Howman were still Builder and Contractors in Sheep Street, Stow on the Wold.

Jessie never married. The death of Gertrude Jessie Howman was registered in the first quarter of 1971 aged 76 in Cheltenham registration district.

Mrs Wixey

Cecil Sharp visited Mrs Wixey, aged 90, on 6 April 1909 at Buckland when she sang him the well-known ballad *Geordie* and songs of young love *Rosetta* and *A Sailor Courted a Farmer's Daughter*. Percy Grainger also visited Mrs Wixey 'aged 77' at Buckland on 31 July 1909 when, as well as Geordie, she sang the tales of young love, *Bold Bonny Boy* and *British Man O' War*.

Mrs Wixey was born Ann Tand(e)y on 22 Jan 1819 in Buckland, the daughter of Joseph and Mary Tandy. Joseph was an agricultural labourer born in Childswickam and Mary was born in Stanton. She had at least three brothers and sisters, Thomas born 1809, Sarah born 1811 and Mary Ann born 1823, all born in Buckland. She married Thomas Best, a labourer, on 22 November 1845 in Buckland. Joseph signed the register and Ann and witness Sarah Tandy, probably Ann's sister, signed by mark. *(Fig 66)*

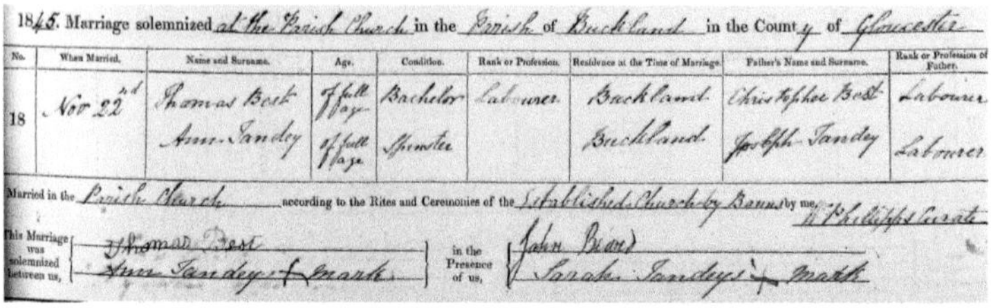
1845. Marriage solemnized at the Parish Church in the Parish of Buckland in the County of Gloucester

No.	When Married.	Name and Surname.	Age.	Condition.	Rank or Profession.	Residence at the Time of Marriage.	Father's Name and Surname.	Rank or Profession of Father.
18	Nov 22nd	Thomas Best	of full age	Bachelor	Labourer	Buckland	Christopher Best	Labourer
		Ann Tandey	of full age	Spinster		Buckland	Joseph Tandey	Labourer

Married in the Parish Church according to the Rites and Ceremonies of the Established Church by Banns by me, W Phillipps Curate

This Marriage was solemnized between us, Thomas Best, Ann Tandey + mark

in the Presence of us, John Beard, Sarah Tandey's + mark

Fig. 66.

By 1851 Ann was working as a glover and living in Buckland with two children, Thomas born 1846 and Mary Ann born 1848. Although Ann was stated to be 'married' Thomas was not in the house at the time of the census. At that time Ann's father, Joseph, was still an agricultural labourer and living in Buckland with his wife and daughter, Sarah, who was also working as an agricultural labourer. By 1861 Ann had moved in with her sister, Sarah, and mother, Mary, in Buckland with her children, Thomas and Mary Ann.

On 31 July 1869 Ann, then a widow, remarried in Buckland to Henry Wixey, a widower and labourer who was born in Kineton, near Temple Guiting and was living in Barton, Guiting Power. Both signed the register by mark. On the same day, and also in Buckland Church, her daughter, Mary Ann, married Henry Irish, a labourer from Buckland who was born in Rous Lench, Worcestershire. *(Figs 67 and 68.)*

Figs. 67 & 68.

By 1871 Ann and Henry were living in Temple Guiting, where Henry was working as an agricultural labourer, with Henry's three children, presumably from a former marriage,

John aged 15, Ann aged 9 and Joseph aged 6, all born in Barton, just outside Temple Guiting. By 1881 Ann and Henry, an agricultural labourer, were still living in Barton, Temple Guiting. The only child remaining at home with them was Henry's son, Joseph. By 1891 Ann and Henry Wixey were living on their own in Barton, Temple Guiting as Joseph Wixey had also left home by then. In 1901 Ann Wixey, a widow, was living with her daughter, Mary Ann's family in Buckland. She died aged 92 and was buried 13 October 1910 in Buckland.

MRS WIXEY'S CHILDREN

Ann's daughter, Mary Ann Irish, after her wedding to Henry Irish on 31 July 1869 had a daughter, Lucy, who was baptised on 12 December 1869 at Buckland. In 1871 they were living in Wormington where Mary Ann was working as an agricultural labourer and her husband, Henry, as a carter. By 1881 Mary Ann Irish, had moved back to Buckland with her husband, Henry, who was working as a farm labourer and they then had three children, Emily baptised 11 August 1872, Edmund baptised 21 November 1875 and Henry Thomas baptised 23 March 1879. They then had another two sons, George baptised 18 June 1882 and William baptised 27 May 1888. All the children were baptised in Buckland. Mary Ann and Henry were still in Buckland in 1901. Their son, Henry Thomas Irish was still living at home and he and his father were both working as ordinary agricultural labourers. Ann Wixey was visiting them and by then was a widow. In 1911 Mary Ann was still living in Buckland where her husband, Henry was working as an agricultural labourer. They had been married for 42 years and had 6 children of whom four were still alive. Mary Ann died in 1939 in Cheltenham.

Mary Ann's daughter, Emily Irish, had left home by 1891 and was working for William and Mary Ann Baker as a general domestic servant at Mount Pleasant Farm in Childswickham.

Emily married William John Farman, a labourer born in Lyttleton, Worcestershire and living at the time at 5 Jakeman Walk, Balsall Heath. They were married in Balsall Heath, Birmingham on 10 September 1899. At the time she was living at 5 Vicarage Road Edgbaston. By 1901 Emily was living in Spungfield Avenue, Balsall Heath with her husband William whose work was laying water pipes. They had also taken in a boarder, David Andrews, also a water pipe layer. In 1911 Emily was still living in Balsall Heath at 2 Back, 48 Wenman St, with her husband who was then working as an inspector in the Corporation water department. They had been married for 10 years and had no children. Emily died in 1945 in Birmingham.

In 1901 Mary Ann's son, Edmund Irish, married Maud Sophia Packer, born in Halesowen, in the Evesham registration district and that year they were living at Fir Tree Hill, Charlecote St Leonard with Maud's brother, George Packer, also born in Halesowen and Maud's sister, Ellen Packer, born in Broadway. Edmund was working as a cowman on a farm and George as an agricultural labourer. By1911 Edmund and Maud had moved back to Buckland with three children, Violet Annie born 1907 and Ellen Maud born 1909. Both children were born in the Winchcombe registration district. Edmund was working as a farm labourer. Violet Anne married William H Reavenall in 1926 in Coventry and died there in 1992. Ellen married Frederick Wankling also in Coventry in 1942. Ellen died in Penzance in 1999 and Edmund died in 1954 in the Warwick registration district.

After his mother married Henry Wixey, Ann's son, **(Henry) Thomas Irish,** stayed in Buckland and was living there in 1871 with his aunt, Sarah Tandy. He married Irene Lodge at the end of 1905 in the Upton on Severn registration district. By 1911 they were living in Buckland where Henry Thomas was working as a bricklayer's labourer. They had one daughter, Irene, born in 1907 in Buckland. They also had a boarder, Henry Troughton, a carter. Irene, died on 1 May 1965 while living at The Lane, Buckland. Probate was granted to Henry Thomas, then described as a retired estate worker. Henry Thomas Irish died later the same year in Cheltenham.

Mrs Packer

Percy Grainger visited **Mrs Packer** who had been a grocer in Stanton and wife of an agricultural labourer on 4 April 1908 when she sang the songs *Erin's Lovely Home, Green Mossy Banks Of The Lee, Lord Bateman, Polly Oliver* and *The Three Gypsies*. He returned on 6 April 1908 when she sang *Mary And The Silvery Tide* and *There Is An Alehouse*.

Mrs Packer was born Jane Holmes in Stanton about 1837, the daughter of Thomas and Sarah Holmes. Thomas was an agricultural labourer, the son of William Holmes from Stanton and his wife, Ann, from Snowshill and was baptised in Stanton on 7 March 1802. The family were representative of an agricultural family who remained in the same location and had many children as shown in the following family history chart. *(Fig 69)*

William had at least two brothers and sisters, George born 1808 and Ann Hannah born 1811. As well as Jane's father, Thomas William and Ann had seven other children, all born in Stanton. Jane was one of eleven children born between 1827 and 1849. By 1841 Jane Holmes was living in Stanton with her family and in 1851 she was still living at home working as a farm labourer as were her brothers, John and Alfred. Her father, Thomas, was also working as an agricultural labourer. Jane married [Ernest] William Packer in 1856 in the Winchcombe registration district which included Stanton. Ernest William Packer had been born in 1829 in Coln St Aldwyns, the son of William and Hosiah Packer and he, his

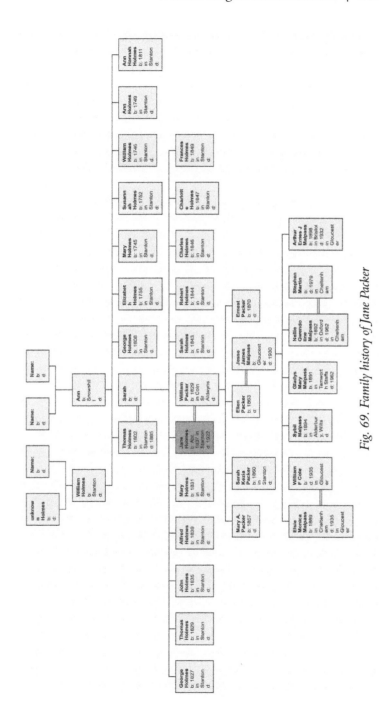

Fig. 69. Family history of Jane Packer

father and two brothers had all been working as agricultural labourers in Coln St Aldwyns in 1851.

By 1861 William and Jane Packer were living in Stanton where William was working as a carter, and they had two children, Mary A. Packer born about 1857 and Sarah Kezia Packer born 1860, both born in Stanton. Jane's parents continued to live in Stanton and by 1861 the only children still living at home with them were Charles and Frances, now called Fanny. In 1871 William and Jane were still living in Stanton where William was working as a labourer and they had two more children, Ellen born about 1863 and Ernest born about 1870. By 1881 they were living in Bank Cottage, Stanton, where William was working as a carter and Jane as a laundress. Their daughter, Ellen, was still living at home and working as a domestic servant and their son, Ernest, was still a scholar. Jane's father, Thomas, then a widower, was living in a cottage in Stanton and died in 1885. William and Jane continued to live in Stanton where William was working as a labourer in 1891 while his son, Ernest, became a gardener. By 1901, however, they were living in the grocer's shop in Stanton where Jane had become the grocer and William continued to work as an agricultural labourer, Their daughter, Sarah Kezia was living with them at that time and working as a dressmaker. Jane Packer died in 1922 in the Winchcombe registration district.

The next generation became more mobile and in about 1887 Jane's daughter, Ellen married Jesse J. Malpass, a commercial traveller and tea merchant born in Gloucester. A daughter, Elsie Monica Malpass, was born to them in Cheltenham in 1889. They then started moving around the country. By 1891, Ellen, now called Helen, and Jesse were living at 4 Victoria Terrace, Bolehall Glascote, Tamworth in Staffordshire and that year they had another daughter, Gladys Mary Malpass, born in Tamworth. At the time of the 1891 census Jesse was working as a 'shopman' and Jane's sister, Kezia, was staying with them. Kezia was single and working as a dressmaker. A further daughter, Nellie Gwen Malpass, was born to Helen and Jesse in Oxford about 1892 and another daughter, Sybil Irene Malpass, was born in Alderbury, Wiltshire in 1894. They then had a son, Arthur Ernest J. Malpass, who was born in Barton Regis, Bristol in 1898. In 1911, Helen and Jesse were living at 36, Sidney Street, Gloucester with Elsie Monica, who was working as a dressmaker, Gladys Mary who was a milliner, Nellie Giben and Sybil Irene who were both shop assistants.

It appears that Helen's son, Arthur Ernest, did not marry as records show that Arthur Ernest William Jesse Malpass of 52 Jersey Road, Gloucester died 4 May 1932 when probate was given to his sister, Nellie Gwendolin Malpass.

Helen's daughter, Elsie Monica Malpass, married William Frank Cole in Gloucester in 1916. William Frank Cole of 18 Derby Road, Gloucester died 2 February 1935 when probate was given to Elsie Monica Cole. Elsie M. Cole died in 1935.

Helen's daughter, Nellie Gwendoline Malpass, was living at 20 Greenway Gardens, Hendon in 1931 and 1932. She married Stephen Martin in Gloucester in 1936. Nellie Martin, formerly Malpass, died in Cheltenham in 1962 and Stephen Martin died in Cheltenham in 1979.

Fig. 70. Stephen Martin, Husband of Nellie Malpass

We have seen that the women of Gloucestershire have sung a variety of traditional songs but what traditional music have the women of Gloucestershire played?

BEATRICE HILL

The song collector Russell Wortley encountered **Beatrice Hill née Bishop, Emily Bishop's sister,** in 1956/7 at Bromsberrow Heath, a village in Gloucestershire but with an address outside the County because of the location of the nearest Postal Sorting Office. Beatrice Hill's father, who came originally from Gloucester, kept the Bell public house in Bromsberrow Heath and was the Morris "King".

Beatrice was a melodeon player. She played country dance tunes and she learned to play the local Morris dance tunes on the melodeon from an earlier team's concertina-player. She played Russell Wortley the traditional dance tunes *A Nutting We Will Go, Down The Middle, The Girl With the Blue Dress On, Jack Robinson, Nelly's Tune, The Three-Handed Reel* and an untitled tune now known widely as *Beatrice Hill's Three Handed Reel*. She also sang him *Annie Lee, Lansdown Fair, Little Pigs, The Londonderry Air, Lord Lovel* and *Maggie*.

Fig. 71. Beatrice Hill
Photo: Cambridge Morris Archives

Peter Kennedy also recorded three of Beatrice Hill's tunes when he was working for the BBC: *Herefordshire Breakdown, Nelly's Tune* and *A Nutting We Will Go*.

Beatrice (Beatie) had left home by 1901 and was working as a housemaid at The Mead, Cirencester (next to the Vicarage) in the household of Wilfred J. Cripps, a barrister and expert on antique plate from an old Cirencester wool family.

Fig 72 The Mead Cirencester in 1901.
Beatie is seated 4th from left middle row.
Photo: Hill family

In 1907 she married Frederick Hill, a labourer and seventh child of Hiram & Ann Hill from Bromsberrow. Shortly afterwards in the same year she had a son, Vivian Allan Hill. Vivian Hill probably married Florence E R Pike in 1946 in the Gloucester Rural registration district and died in 1988 in Gloucester.

In 1911 Beatrice and Frederick were living at Rock Cottage, Ryton, Dymock and had another son, Ivor, born about 1909. A family tree on www.ancestry.com also refers to a further son, Carroll Hill who died in 2001. In 1922 Beatrice and Frederick had a daughter, Frances Thelma M. Hill.

Beatrice Hill died 19 February 1963 in Gloucester Royal Hospital. Her address then was given as Homestead, Bromsberrow Heath, near Ledbury. Probate was given to her son, Vivian Alan Hill, who was a cemetery worker.

Fig. 73.
Beatrice Bishop
early 1900s
Photo: Hill family

Fig. 74. A melodeon which
belonged to Beatrice Hill.

Beatrice's daughter, Thelma, married Douglas G. Hill in 1946 in the Gloucester Rural registration district. Douglas G. Hill died in Gloucestershire on 8 December 2003 and Thelma on December 2012 in Bromsberrow. [26]

The Holly And The Ivy

The holly hath the berry as red as any blood
And merry rose sweet Jesus Christ for to do poor sinners good.

(Chorus) The rising of the sun and the running of the deer
The playing of the merry organ, sweet singing in the choir

The holly hath a prickle as sharp as any thorn
And merry rose sweet Jesus Christ on Christmas Day in the morn.
Chorus

The holly and the ivy when they are both full grown,
But of all the trees that are in the wood the holly bears the crown.
Chorus

Source: Sung by Mrs Mary Ann Clayton (64) , Chipping Campden. Collected by Cecil Sharp, 13 January 1909

©Gloucestershire Traditions

Annie Lee

I've writ - ten him a let - - ter to tell him he is free,

And this mo - ment and for ev - - er he is no - thing more to me,

My heart is light and gay, _____ for since the deed is done

I'll let him know when court - ing, he should on - ly court but one.

I'll let him know when court - ing, he should on - ly court but one.

Variant verse 2

cant-ered by his side, Yes! and I'll

2. All the people in the village knew that he was courting me,
   And this morning he went riding with that saucy Annie Lee.
   And they said he smiled upon her as she cantered by his side,
   Yes! and I'll warrant he has promised to make her soon his bride. (Repeat last line)

3. At twilight in the evening he said he'd visit me,
   But no doubt he's still with Annie, and he can be with her for me.
   For sure as I am living if he comes here any more
   I'll look as though we never, no, never met before. (Repeat last line)

4. It is time he should be coming. Oh! I wonder if he will.
   If he does I'll look as cool - what's that shadow on the hill?
   It is someone in the moonlight, it is someone drawing near,
   Yes! and it is his figure just as true as I am here. (Repeat last line)

5. Now I am sorry I have written to tell him he is free,
   No doubt it was a story that he rode with Annie Lee.
   He is coming through the gateway and I'll meet him at the door,
   And I'll tell him I still loves him if he'll court Miss Lee no more. (Repeat last line)

Source: Beatrice Hill, Bromsberrow Heath, 27th August 1957, collected by Russell Wortley

© Gloucestershire Traditions

6

SINGERS OF COMIC SONGS

Like most country folk, most traditional Gloucestershire singers had at least one comic song in their repertoire to lighten the evening. In the older repertoire, these might have been songs about mishaps in married life, from boisterous adultery and seduction to the pitfalls of marrying an old man, and in the later repertoires, all sorts of influences including from the music halls. These latter songs often contained thinly disguised erotic innuendo, from the Clockmender who liked winding up ladies' clocks to the more agricultural 'winding up her ball of yarn' or 'showing her the works of my thrashing machine.' Some other comic songs were parodies of well-known popular songs such as *Old Joe Whip*, a rewriting of the American song *Casey Jones*. The paragraphs that follow tell of some of the singers and the comic songs in their repertoire.

In the case of some singers, most of their repertoire consisted of comic songs, and so it is hard to pick out just one or two items. Such was the case with **Ray Hartland** of Eldersfield. Ray was a well-known character in the area, both as a farmer and as an entertainer in pubs and concert parties. Ray was in his fifties when visited by Carol and Gwilym Davies in 1978 to record his songs. Later, Gwilym and Carol took Mike Yates to meet him and make further recordings.

Raymond Jack Hartland *(Fig 75)* was born in Haw Bridge on 7 March 1923. His father, John Hartland, worked on the river barges but died when Ray was 9. His mother, Lucy, worked on the land to support her children, Ray and his siblings Bill, Phyllis and Daphne. (Lucy later remarried a butcher, William C. Betteridge, in 1944 and both died in 1974, William aged 100.) Ray started school at the tender age of three and a half at Tirley and by the age of 14 he was working at Tirley Court, helping out after school at Flat Farm, Tirley working for Arthur Strawford. In 1952 Ray married Arthur's daughter Betty Strawford and sometime between 1965 and 1968 took over the running of Flat farm. Their son David was born in 1957 and Dereck in 1960.

Fig. 75.

Figs. 76 & 77. Ray and Betty's Wedding 1951

Ray farmed cattle at Flat Farm but when he was not out tending the herd, he turned to his great passion, i.e. making cider, which he had been doing from the age of 13. His cider barn at Flat Farm housed 300 gallon kegs of home-made cider of varying sweetnesses and quality, making up to 6,000 gallons a year. He kept Kingston Black apples for his best brew. He was also adept at making perry (cider from pears) which is said to be the 'real' Gloucestershire cider, and Plum Jerkin. The song collectors mentioned above were delighted to be served scrumpy in cow's-horn cups, but politely declined a pinch of snuff. At weekends, the cider barn would be a meeting place for Ray and his friends, singing songs and carrying out quality control on the various liquid refreshments available.

In whatever spare time he had, he had been a bellringer at Tirley Church and played cricket for Tirley and Hasfield. During the War he was a member of the Home Guard.

Ray died in 1996 and at his funeral the church was filled with family and friends and reference was made to his immense character, his amazing understanding and how he was a man who made people laugh and brought pleasure to many. Bishop Robin Wood, former Bishop of Worcester described him as 'Of true Gloucestershire stock with twinkling eyes and a wonderful complexion.'

Happily Ray's son Dereck has taken on the cider-making mantle, moving to nearby Tirley Villa with five acres and more land rented. Hartland's Farmhouse Cider can still be bought in the area and over the years has won awards, such as at the 1989 Great British Beer Festival at Norwich and at the Big Apple Cider Trials at Putley.

As a singer and entertainer, Ray was never short of a song and most of his repertoire reflected his jolly personality, his rural background and his sometime wicked sense of humour. Some the songs he knew were:

Buttercup Joe

The Fisher's Boy (a Parody of *The Farmer's Boy*)

Three Men went a-Hunting

I wish I was Single Again

The Old Sow, (which requires a certain amount of verbal agility*)*

The Pub with No Beer

Twelve Stone Two – a rare music hall song

Ball of Yarn

Billy Johnson's Ball – about a christening party that got out of hand

My Husband's a Sailor – armed forces bawdiness

All delivered with a rich Gloucestershire twang.[27]

Fig. 78. Betty and Ray with Grandchild

One of Ray's songs, *The Ball of Yarn*, a thinly-disguised tale of seduction, was also a favourite of gypsy singer **Danny Brazil** from Staverton (Footnote: see chapter on gypsy singers for more information on the Brazil family) and also the singer, *Billy Buckingham* under the name of *the Little Ball of Twine*. Gwilym Davies recorded **William (Billy) Buckingham** singing *The Waysailing Bowl, Come In The Parlour Charlie, My Father's Name Was Adam* and *A Group Of Young Soldiers* in February 1979 at the Royal Arms in Stonehouse and later on 13 February 1999 Gwilym and Carol Davies videoed him singing the Waysailing Bowl and talking about the custom.

Fig. 79. Billy Buckingham

Billy Buckingham was born circa 1902 and at age 8 moved to Kingscourt, near Stroud. He had two sons and a daughter. As a boy, he learnt the local version of the *Waysailing Bowl* and he and his companions, including his uncle, Albert, would travel around the local farms and big houses singing the song and collecting money. On a good night, they would make £3 each. In the 1970s, Billy would entertain regulars in the Spa Hotel and the now defunct Royal Arms in Stonehouse, with his version of the wassail song along with other songs such as the *Little Ball of Twine* and *As I Came Home*. William James Buckingham died in June 2003 aged 91.

RUSTIC COMIC SONGS

Comic songs about agriculture were well appreciated by the listeners. One recurrent theme is songs about crows, the bane of a farmer's life. These days, we are more distanced from what a crow represents. To us it is just a big black bird but to the agricultural community it was a scourge: it was the bird that stole the farmer's corn, his very livelihood, from the ground and then sat in a tree gloating about it. They were pests to be shot.

For example **George Edward Hill** of Dursley in 1934, sang *The Tailor and the Carrion Crow* where the farmer shoots at the crow only to hit his pig instead. Bear in mind that tailoring was not a respected profession in farming communities and so the fact that the tailor was a poor shot would be no surprise to the audience. The humour of the song may sound a little thin today but the audiences would have enjoyed singing along.

We know that George Edward Hill was born in Dursley in January 1872 and that in 1893 he married a girl from nearby Uley, Annie Elizabeth Hurn. The couple lived in the hamlet of Woodmancote, near Dursley and went on to have seven children, three sons and four daughters. George died in 1944, aged 72.

We also know a little of his background from Richard Childlaw's researches. His daughter, Frances, said that her father used to play the accordion at the Albert Hall and got a guinea a minute broadcasting at Birmingham on the radio. He used to be a bandmaster and took a room down the YMCA (Long Street, Dursley) with Frances and her brother and taught a lot of young people to dance. There were others in the band: Charlie Webb, Bill Hill, and Gunner Smith.

Fig. 80. George Hill.
Photo: Mr Cecil Pyle – D.E. Evans Collection

George learned his songs from his mother who lived in two houses at the bottom of Hunger Hill with loads of garden and fruit bushes. George's mother was born Mary Ann Whittard (1828 – 1901) the daughter of John and Alice Whittard of Dursley. Her father was a mason who died young. She was a wire-setter, working for George Lister at Rivers Mill, Dursley. (This was before the business became R.A. Lister.) On the 24 April 1846, she was caught stealing half a pound of butter and was sentenced to 6 weeks hard labour at Horsley House of Correction. She was 5ft 4inches, with brown hair, grey eyes, and a long face much pitted with smallpox. She had never been in gaol before. Her conduct was orderly and she attended the Wesleyan chapel in Dursley. (She lived next door to the Wesleyan Manse in May Lane.)

George's father was a baker, but unlike one of his brothers who carried on the bakery business, George joined his brother Samuel in the blacksmith trade in Dursley. George's sisters took on the typical work of the area – girls were cloth weavers, wool spinners and pin makers. We also know that he was a self-taught musician with experience of brass bands. So what with smithying and music, George must have been a well-known character in the area.

In 1934, the English Folk dance and Song Society (EFDSS) was in momentum, carrying on from the heritage of Cecil Sharp and setting up regional committees. The local Society representative and teacher was a Miss Clare Newhouse. Miss Newhouse had taught folk dancing in Oxford before coming to Gloucestershire so she would have been active in the Dursley area, promoting English song and dance. It was perhaps by chance that George Hill attended an event she had organised and on hearing *"One man shall mow my meadow"* the thought came to him that he had some songs to contribute and so he sang half a dozen songs to Miss Newhouse, even though *"not a note had been in his head for fifty years"*, i.e. back to his childhood.

Two of these songs were published by EFDSS in 1934, but it seems that the other songs are lost. It must have been a matter of considerable pride to know that one of his songs *"A Bowl, A Bottle"* was sung by the Gloucestershire team at the All England Festival in the Albert Hall on January 5th, 1934.

MORE CROWS

One of the most popular songs in Gloucestershire, and sung in various forms, was *'There Were Two Crows'* as sung by **Charlie Clissold.** The song itself can be traced back to the 17th century *Three Ravens*, a mysterious tale in which a pregnant doe buries a mortally wounded knight (how?) before dying herself. This is perhaps an allegory of love and devotion but by the time the song found a place in rural Gloucestershire, and had been around the globe with corners knocked off, the song was simply a piece of rural nonsense, the farmer and his eternal battle with the crows eating his crops and flying off to taunt the farmer. In some cases, including Charlie's version, the song became a vehicle for some Anglo-Saxon expletives which with the right audience would have had the requisite comic effect.

Fig. 81. Charlie Clissold.
(Photo courtesy of Mrs E. Clissold)

Charlie himself was a member of a long-established Gloucestershire farming family and the surname is found predominantly in the county. Charlie and his brother grew up in Moreton Valence and never moved far away from that area. Charlie however, left the farm, rented it out and then worked for the council. He was a well-known local character with a rich Gloucestershire 'burr' and was always ready to give a song in the pubs. A visit to his house would be sure to be accompanied by his home-made fruit wine. He very much favoured comic songs, some rather risqué, and knew a host of music hall ditties. Another of his songs *The Ledbury Clergyman* tells the comic story, apparently true, of a vicar involved in a paternity case. In 1977, Carol and Gwilym Davies recorded him in his home and the folklorist Mike Yates made subsequent recordings. Mike described him as a real character.

RUSTIC SELF-PARODY

It is perhaps surprising that people are so willing to sing songs which are parodies of themselves. A vogue grew up in many places for songs about the rustic, clod-hopping bumbling farmer, ignorant of all worldly matters except their little village and farming, awkward with the opposite sex and speaking and singing in broad dialect. Yet among this self-parody we sometimes get streaks of worldly wisdom which the country dweller possesses and which his/her urban counterpart does not. Many such songs arose, probably out of the music hall tradition, which were taken up by country singers to the delight of audiences in village hall or pub. Songs of this ilk would be *Buttercup Joe, I Bain't half so Soft as I looks, Down in the Field where the Buttercups all Grow*, and so on.

A very typical song in this genre is *Varmer Giles* by Gilbert Wells and T F Robson and published in 1902, as sung by **David Gardner** of Tresham and others.

Fig. 82. David Gardner.
Photo – Gwilym Davies

David came to the attention of folk song collectors when he went up to two local well-known folk performers after one of their concerts and asked why they didn't sing "some of the old Gloucestershire songs". He was subsequently visited by Gwilym Davies who recorded his songs, stories and his harmonica playing. David's son Mike Gardner is carrying on the family musical tradition and is singing his father's songs.

David was born on 28 September 1924 in Tresham. He played the melodeon at 6 years of age, learnt the piano as a child and played the church organ. He learned songs as a boy from farm labourers and took every opportunity to travel on the farm carts with them, or to go hunting rabbits. He attended the grammar school in Wotton Under Edge and then went to work as an apprentice engineer at the R. A. Lister company of Dursley.

During WWII he joined up 'in the thick of things' and was in 21st Army group during the British occupation of the Rhine during which he was recognised for his bravery under heavy enemy fire when he rescued a severely injured officer. He also used his shooting skills as a sniper and was involved at D Day in 'Monty's own Division'. He also learnt songs from his army friends during the war. One of his songs was a humorous recruiting song, the *Gloucester Blinder*.

After the war he returned to engineering and married a local girl, Margaret, on 25 December 1948, in Kensington. He continued to sing and play guitar, piano accordion, harmonica, piano and organ around local pubs, clubs and gatherings, forming a skiffle group called 'The Ragtime Rascals' who appeared on a Television talent show called " Now's Your Chance" in the late 1950s. After he was 'discovered' by the folk world, David appeared at several small events, singing his songs, usually to guitar accompaniment. He died just short of his 90th birthday in 2013.

Another old Gloucestershire singer was **Tony Ballinger** who with his father used to frequent the King's Head at Upton-St-Leonards, which in the 70s was a lively local with much atmosphere and singing. Gwilym Davies met Tony there in 1977 and recorded several songs and fragments from him in the noisy bar. Gwilym subsequently met up with Tony in the Brockworth House Club and recorded further songs. Tony was very much a local man whose trade was machine setter. His descendants still live in Brockworth.

One of Tony's favourite songs was one generally known as *The Swapping song* with the unlikely chorus:

With a wing wang waddle-oh, Jack sold his saddle-oh
Flossy boy, bubble-oh, under the moon.

The song tells of a country boy who through buying and selling manages to lose all his money: starting with a plough, he swaps it for a cow, a calf, a dog, a cat and a mouse. The mouse somehow manages to burn down the house. This comic theme is very old and is found in other European countries. It is still sung in the area: the well-known singer Ken Langsbury learnt a version from his mother.

Arthur Ellaway lived in Charlton Kings and was of some renown as a local singer. His family came from Lydney via Newport, Monmouthshire and Chepstow. He was born in Lydney in 1902, brought up by his grandparents, and always regarded himself as a 'forester'. He was blind from birth and took up the trade of basket-making. In 1932 he married Susan Cook of Charlton Kings and they had two sons, Gerald and David. In his younger days he loved singing parlour songs such as *Old Father Thames* and *Bless this House*, with a fine tenor voice. He was also a great raconteur of dialect stories, usually concerning the rustic hero Shadrack Cowmeadow. Being blind from birth, music was one of the delights of his life, along with making potent home-made beer, and he would record his songs onto a reel-to-reel tape recorder. Apart from his parlour songs, he had a number of comic songs, including the rare *Somerset Fair* which, despite its title, he regarded as a Forest of Dean song.

The song *Somerset Fair* which has only been found in Gloucestershire and East Anglia, is probably the product of the music hall, although no original sheet music can be traced. In the song, the various delights of the fair are enumerated, from the saucy young lady showing her underwear as she swings, to the fat lady, the boxer and the greasy pole. At one time it was a regular feature at country fairs for there to be a greasy pole and whoever could climb it would be sure of a prize, in this case a side of bacon.

SONGS OF COURTING AND SEDUCTION

Throughout the ages and in all lands, love and marriage has

always been an object of humour. Courtship can also be the source of comedy, with the clumsy suitor, or even, in some cases, the married man courting the young lady (what a cad). A streak of jolly bawdiness also runs through society and whilst it can shock, it can also delight.

We have already mentioned rustic parodies and a song which covers that category is *Down in the Fields where the Buttercups all Grow*. This was recorded on a 78 rpm record by one Charlie Higgins in 1931 and was soon taken up by singers up and down the country.

One of those singers was **Ken Langsbury** from Cheltenham. As people will testify, no-one can put over a rustic song in the way Ken does and he is in great demand for his characterful singing. Ken is a printer by trade and although not Gloucestershire born, he has lived here since early childhood and his rich Gloucestershire voice is well-known. In the 70s, the trio "The Songwainers", of which he was a member, achieved national acclaim. He is also a sponge for songs and throughout his life he has learnt songs from family, friends, gypsies, the armed forces and so on.

The song *Down in the Fields where the Buttercups all Grow* is a typical product of the late music hall, poking gentle fun at the rustic suitor trying to carry out his romantic courting in a countryside full of obstacles such as vegetation, cattle, bees and unhygienic songbirds. Whereas earlier songs treated females with great respect as creatures of grace and beauty, in this song, the unfortunate girl is 'bandy-legged'. But all is well that ends well and the field of buttercups proves a better place for their canoodling than the marriage bed.

In a different category is the humour of *Oh Soldier, will you Marry me* collected by Hurlbutt Albino (1889-1957) from his father **Henry Charles Albino**. On the face of it, this is an innocent enough song of the girl providing clothes for her fiancé only to find out in the last verse that he has a wife already. In some circumstances this might be a serious ballad but the gentle repetition and the easily remembered verses make it a light-hearted romp.

The Albino family was of Italian extraction. Henry Charles Albino's father was Vitore Albino who was born in Italy, the son of Bosano Albino, a farmer, who came to live in England. Vitore set up as a jeweller in Bourton on the Water and married Eliza Wilson on 19 May 1842, a merchant's daughter. Their son Henry Charles Albino received an expensive education at Cheltenham College: in 1871 he was one of 14 boarders at Birdlip House, St Luke's, Cheltenham. After Henry left school and after the death of his father he went to work for his mother Eliza in Leicester where Eliza kept the Cricket Players Inn at 3 and 5 Church Gate, St Margaret's, Leicester. In 1886 Henry married Mary Jane Ann Hurlbutt from Bourton on the Water. Their son Harry was born in 1890, and the following year the couple moved to 1 Compton Terrace, Vicar's Moon Lane, Edmonton, London. The family added further children to their name, moving around to Brighton and then back to London. Henry's occupation was then described as 'merchant'. He probably moved back to Bourton on the Water as he was buried there in 1925.

Thus it can be seen that unlike most traditional singers who were from an agricultural background, Harry's was quite different. He was probably bilingual, educated and a businessman. Their family experience at running a city pub probably gave them a good insight into vernacular culture. Henry and Mary ensured that their son Harry had a similarly good education and attended Cambridge University. With this colourful and cultured background, young Harry developed a host of interests such as vernacular architecture, wagons, millstones and of course folk music, so what more natural than that Harry should turn to his colourful father for old songs. Despite the fact that his father had moved around so much in his life and had such a varied background, he still recognised his songs as Gloucestershire folksongs.

Most people will know the song *No, John, No* from their schooldays. The 'trick' of the words is that the lady's answer of 'No' to her suitor's advances eventually becomes the equivalent of 'Yes'. **Emily Bishop** from Bromsberrow Heath sang a version of this song. Many of Emily's songs were religious ones on Christian themes but she also had a number of old folk songs and ballads in her repertoire. (More information on Emily and her background is given in Chapter 5 Women Singers.)

A situation which in some cases would be serious can became comic – it all depends on what slant is given to them. The situation of a girl getting pregnant but concealing the fact, and then her father finding out when the infant starts crying could be classed as traumatic for all concerned and certainly this is probably how the song *Underneath her Apron* started life. However, at some time in its life, the song acquired a jaunty, flippant music hall type tune and some 'nudge, nudge, wink, wink' words and phrases which turn it into a comic song, in the right company, that is.

This was the song sung by the Gloucestershire gypsy **Danny Brazil**. Danny was a remarkable source for songs, mostly learnt from his family. Many were old ballads on serious themes, but Danny had a quiet sense of humour and a number of comic songs. (More about Danny and his life can be found in Chapter 4 Gypsy singers.)

DECEIVED HUSBANDS

The theme of the unfortunate cuckold has long been a source of humour, not only in England but in many folk cultures. The humour is heightened when the adulterer gets his (usually his) come-uppance in a humorous way. There are many songs of this theme in the English tradition and one that has persisted over many centuries is the song often known as *Seven Nights Drunk*, even though many versions do not get as far as seven verses for the days of the week. This song is still sung in many versions to this day, almost always to the delight of the audience. The succession of discarded clothing and the suspicious but gullible husband's progress throughout the house and up to the bedroom still brings a smile to all but the humourless.

One version of this song was sung by **Ray Hartland** of Tirley. In Ray's version, there is an added strand to the humour in the broad Gloucestershire dialect in which it is sung. A further song about a disgruntled husband sung by Ray Hartland was *I Wish I Was Single Again.* (For more information on Ray, see above)

The song *The Croppy Tailor* is typical of a number of songs in which the adulterer, invariably male, has to hide when the husband returns unexpectedly and usually gets found out in hilarious circumstances. Very often, the situation arises when the husband is away at sea. In this case, the villain is found out when the husband decides to burn the cupboard in which the lover is hiding. As in many other folk songs, the tailor is the one who comes off worse – in this case by having his ears clipped (hence 'croppy') – but at least in this tale he had the consolation of having had his wicked way with the sailor's wife.

Such was the song sung by **Danny Brazil,** the gypsy singer from Staverton, whom we have already met, with the song *Underneath her Apron.* (see chapter on Gypsy singers for more information about the Brazil family).

A similar tale is told in *The German Clockmender.* This song seems to have gained popularity in the 1940s when Germans were not exactly in favour and so a comic song about a lusty clockmaker who goes around the countryside 'winding up ladies' clocks' and eventually being found out would have found popularity. The tale is found in many hundreds of jokes about lecherous milkmen or door-to-door salesmen. English folksong is full of metaphors of sexual activity, and so 'winding her clock' is as effective as any.

Several Gloucestershire singers had versions of this song, including **Jerry Protherough** of Charlton Kings, **Dick Parsons** of Shurdington and **David Gardner** from Tresham, of whom we have spoken above.

Jerry Protherough came from a well-established Charlton Kings family which goes back there to the early 19th century and probably earlier. There is a record of one James Protherough, cobbler, and his Welsh wife raising a family of six children in Charlton Kings from 1829 onwards in the very district in which Jerry lived and so it is probable that his family went back several generations in that area. Jerry himself had been a keen singer – disability had dimmed his voice a little but not his enthusiasm for his songs, even though he was wheelchair-bound in his latter days. He told the collector Gwilym Davies that he had been a keen gardener for decades and that his vegetables were planted with military precision. The 1829 family mentioned above included laundresses, labourers and gardeners and it is tempting to think that Jerry inherited his love of gardening from those previous generations.

Another Gloucestershire singer who delighted in the song *The German Clockmender* was **Dick Parsons** from the Bentham/ Shurdington area south of Cheltenham. Dick was very much Gloucestershire born and bred and always lived around the area. His rich Gloucestershire speech was always a feature. He was probably born 12 September 1909 and lived with his brother in a caravan in the countryside. When younger, Dick, his brother and others had gone around the area of Shurdington and Hatherley at Christmas time 'waysailing', taking the traditional wassail bowl with them. They used to carry a squeezebox (probably a melodeon) with them, until one day one of the party walked into a lamppost whilst playing the instrument and ended up with half the instrument in each hand! Dick and his friends used to sing at a regular singaround in Dog Lane, Birdlip, in a venue they named "The Rampant Cat", passing round the cider as they went. Dick was a regular at the Cheeserollers pub at Shurdington where he also sang. He died about 1981 aged 71 in Cheltenham.

WOMEN GETTING THE BETTER OF MEN

Several of the comic songs found in Gloucestershire and elsewhere concern specifically women who get the upper hand on men. The song *The Female Cabin Boy* (sometimes known as *The Handsome Cabin Boy)* is well-known in folk song circles and is one of the songs sung to the collector Cecil Sharp in Gloucestershire. This tale brings in the theme of a girl dressing as a man to go away to sea. In many versions of this scenario, the girl is seeking her lover but in this particular song, the girl goes in for cross-dressing on a whim. However, her status is noticed by the ship's captain who has his wicked way with her, with predictable results. As a comic song, it still has the ability to amuse (unlike some earlier comic songs).

So the story is a bit on the cheeky side. When Cecil Sharp visited **Mrs Mary Clayton** at the Thatched Cottage in Sheep Street, Chipping Campden, on 13 January 1909 when she was about 64 years old Mrs Clayton sang him the first verse of *The Female Cabin Boy.* Sharp was not above collecting words of songs that were openly bawdy but it is possible that either he did not note the rest of the words because they were already known to him or else Mrs Clayton chose not to sing the whole song to Sharp through modesty. Who knows?

Disparity of ages is often a cause for merriment, always concerning a young woman who marries an old man. These songs nearly always highlight the inability of the man to satisfy his young wife. In the case of the song *An Old Man came Courting Me'*, the girl seeks such satisfaction in the arms of someone younger. Such was the song as sung by the gypsy **Danny Brazil** (see chapter on gypsy singers for more information on the Brazil family), to a very handsome tune.

This song was also sung by **Ernie Lane**, poet and cricketer of Dumbleton, and was a regular for the after cricket celebrations at Dumbleton cricket club (which used to make its own cider) but in Ernie's version the girl at least returns to her 'sleepy old man' before he can wake up.

Another song, and quite an unusual one, in which the woman gets the better of her man, is *Lobski,* a curious song that owes more to the early music hall then to folk tradition. In this song, the man hopes to deceive his wife by claiming that he was going fishing whereas his real intention was extra-marital amorousness. He is found out when his savvy wife realises that you don't catch sea fish (sprats) from fresh water fishing. How many people these days would spot that obvious mistake?

Fig. 83.

This was the same song that came down in the repertoire of **Archer Goode**. Archer lived many years in Charlton Kings, Cheltenham and had a wide variety of songs. He was originally from Abergavenny, and his speech always retained a Welsh lilt. His family ties went back to the Leominster area of Herefordshire and he was descended from a long line of farm workers. He had worked with horses on rural farms and often spoke of his farming days, writing songs to celebrate working rural life. He retained many old rural skills and in Charlton Kings he earned some money as a repairer and restorer of lawnmowers. In the 1930s he befriended the Warwickshire Morris dancer Sam Bennett and would often hear Sam sing or perform a dance. He learned a number of songs from Sam. Archer's great delight was singing and he had a large repertoire, some songs learnt from his younger days or from his mother and some from old song books, which is possibly where he picked up *Lobski*. After Archer's move to Cheltenham he became a stalwart of the folk clubs. With his wife Janet, Archer had at least one daughter. He died in Cheltenham in 1984.

MUSIC HALL SONGS

The English music halls arose from the 18th century taverns and coffee houses and grew to become musical clubs. They became very popular throughout the 19th century and gave many professional singers and comedians a platform. The songs that went down best at the music hall were comedy songs, often performed in the appropriate costume, or sentimental songs and many of these were rapidly absorbed by the listeners into their own repertoires to sing in family or village gatherings. The music hall audiences delighted in songs that were rather risqué or even on the smutty side. Double entendre was the order of the day, as in such songs as *I'll be Up Her Way Next Week* or *Oh Timothy, Let's Have a Look at It*.

One such song was the wonderfully titled *They're Moving Grandad's Grave to Build a Sewer* as sung by **David Gardner**, whom we have already met (see above). The humour of this song relies on the surreal scenario of Grandad being so affronted by his body being moved to build a sewer that he will haunt the families using the sewer for ever. Presumably Grandad's spirit would have been alright with the authorities moving his body to construct, say a park, but a sewer? I ask you.

The unlikely titled *I'd Rather Lather Father then Father Lather me (Fig 84)* was written in 1876 and recorded by the music hall singer Harry Hemsley and it is probable that this is how the song came down to **Reg Hannis**. The joke of the song is around the double meaning of 'lather' to mean either to soap someone prior to shaving or to give someone a good beating. Do many people these days recognise that second meaning of the word? There is also of course the comic alliteration of the words.

Fig. 84.

Reg was a real Gloucestershire character. The Hannis family goes back many generations in Gloucestershire and the surname is only found in that area. The first known mention of the Hannis family in the area was in 1793 and they subsequently worked there as gardeners, carpenters and gamekeepers. Reg's grandparents had a wood business and ran the local post office and the family continued dealing in wood at Brotheridge Farm in Cranham. Reg inherited his love of wood and his trade was to deal in wood. He was born in 1928 in the secluded Cotswold village of Cranham and lived there all his life. A feature of Reg's speech was his broad Gloucestershire dialect and he often used the word 'thick' for 'this' as well as older forms of words such as cassn't (can't) cussn't (couldn't) or byent (are not). Reg played melodeon and was often found in the local pubs playing and singing, particularly in his local, the Black Horse at Cranham. He was also a great collector of musical instruments and had a fine collection of melodeons, concertinas and accordeons which he kept in his woodshed. Reg died in 1997 but his love of music has been passed on to his son James who is a fine melodeon player and to James' daughter Debra who is an avid singer of folk songs.

Reg's wife **Gwen Hannis** (née Brind) was also a keen singer of songs. They shared some songs in common such as *Buttercup Joe* but Gwen had her own repertoire of songs. One such song is the surreal *Your Baby has Gone down the Plughole*. In this song, the skinny baby's demise is lamented by singing angels but all is well as the baby is 'not lost, just gone before.' So that's all right. No-one really knows where this song came from but it has gone into the Cockney song repertoire.

NONSENSE SONGS

Sometimes people just enjoy hearing songs which are

amusingly nonsensical, perhaps because the situations described therein are fantasy or perhaps because the song is a vehicle for amusing but meaningless wordplay.

Several of the singers previously mentioned in this chapter sang such songs. **Ray Hartland** (see above) had a song called *Three Men Went a-Travelling* where people vie for the most nonsensical description of what they can see before them. This song is known from a seventeenth century broadside called 'A Choice of Inventions' and may even be older and is known in other versions as *Three Jolly Welshman*. Some of the humour depends on the apparent stupidity of the Irishman in the song who always gets hold of the wrong end of the stick. Ray only sang one verse to the collector but in common with other versions of the song it is boisterously scatological.

Folklore is sprinkled with humorous tales of magic or unlikely beasts, from the fabulous Lambton Worm that "grewed an aaful size" to the Wonderful Crocodile that measured 500 mile from nose to tail. One very famous song in this genre is the legendary Derby Ram, which seems to grow bigger in every verse of the song, and which has gone around the world to English rugby clubs, the Appalachian mountains, the wilds of Canada and so on. It is not often found in the repertoire of gypsy singers but **Danny Brazil's** (see above) version of *The Salisbury Ram* is an exception. In fact, although Danny's version starts by singing of Salisbury, the latter verses revert to Derby.

We have already spoken about **David Gardner** in connection with other songs and David certainly did a lot of entertaining in his lifetime. His song *Now Listen all you Sailor Boys* sounds like it is going to be an old sea shanty until we learn the "the wind blew off the captain's wooden leg' and that the ship hit 'a Christmas tree' and the crew 'all fell down a tunnel in the dark'.

One of the oldest nonsense songs in the English repertoire is *Gossip Jones (or 'Joan')*. The humour of this song relies on the notion that when two people are gossiping in the street what they are saying is nonsense, with verses about a sick pig, a drunken wife and hopping off to the gin shop. The song is probably not hilarious to modern audiences but has survived for 300 years and its appeal is in its catchy chorus.

This song was sung in Gloucestershire by **Thomas Lanchbury** of Wyck Rissington. We know quite a lot about Thomas: he was born in Wyck Rissington in 1865 to John Lanchbury, a labourer and Hannah from Castle Eaton in Wiltshire. His first wife Malvinia Webb died within a year of their marriage in 1887 at the age of 28, but in 1902 he married again to Catherine Higgs, a farmer's daughter from Wyck Rissington. The couple continued to live there but had no children. Catherine died in 1933 and Thomas a year later.

Thomas was clearly a very active and musical man. He was a man of the soil, being a cowman by profession. As well as being a bell-ringer, as his father and grandfather had been before, he had a repertoire of old country songs. He remembered the Morris dancers and was able to describe the home made fiddle that supplied the music.

Cumulative Songs

The aforementioned singers **Thomas Lanchbury** and **Ernie Lane** both had cumulative fun songs where everyone could join in, in the vein of Old MacDonald Had a Farm', well suited to life in the countryside. Thomas' song was *Down in the Land of Greeno*, a song similar to the ubiquitous *Old MacDonald Had a Farm*. In fact, *Greeno* is an older version of *MacDonald* and a welcome change. Ernie's song *I went to Market,* which he learnt in the village of Dumbleton from Arthur Sallis, details a series of animals which the singer has bought at market and 'fed him all under a tree'. To the delight of (some of) the audience, he goes to market to buy a wife, but still feeds her under a tree. Both these songs have great scope for making animal noises.

Popular comic songs crossed county boundaries and another song in the repertoire of Thomas Lanchbury was a Gloucestershire version of the well known *Widdicombe Fair*. In Thomas' version, the action is transported to *Stow Fair* and Uncle Tom Cobley has become Uncle Tom Goblin.

I Wish I was Single again

2. Now, my wife she took fever, so then, so then
    My wife she caught fever, so then
    Oh, my wife she caught fever, I hope it won't leave her
    I want to be single again
    Again and again and again, Again and again and again
    Oh, my wife she caught fever
    I hope it wont leave her,
    I want to be single again.

3. Now, my poor wife she died, so then, so then
    My poor wife she died, so then
    Oh, my poor wife she died, and I laughed 'til I cried
    I want to be single again
    Again and again and again, Again and again and again
    And when I was single my pockets did jingle
    I want to be single again.

4. Now, I took to another, so then, so then
   I took to another, so then
   Oh, I took to another, she turned out a bugger
   And I want to be single again
   Again and again and again, Again and again and again
   And when I was single my pockets did jingle
   I want to be single again.

5. So, all you young men who have wives, have wives
   All you young men who have wives
   Take care of the purse 'cos the next may be worse.

   And you'll want to be single again.

Sung by Ray Hartland, Eldersfield. Collected by Gwilym Davies 9
December, 1978 ©Gloucestershire Traditions

*Comic Song from Tirley sung by Ray Hartland to song collector
Gwilym Davies in 1978*

The Gloucester Blinder

1. In Glo' - ster - shire where I comes from they calls I an art-ful old dod-ger,_____ They asked I o'er and o'er a - gain if I could be a sol - dier,_____ They asked I o'er and o'er a - gain if I could take a shin - er,_____ and they Told me that the name of me corps would be The Glo' - ster Blin - der,_____ With a Fa - la - la here and a fa - la - la there, fa - la - la la when I get w'hom.

2. They took I on the square that day, a followin' up the band, sir.
   And a gurt tall chap way out in front, why didn't he thump that drum, sir.
   He'd swing his sticks up over his y'ead, wallop, he brought 'em down, sir.
   And he hut ["hit"] a gurt hole in the side of the drum, as bigger than a mangle wurzle.

3. They took us on parade thuck ["that"] day, doin' our duty manual
   And round and round thuck square we went, as the rifles we did handle
   'Twas eyes right, eyes left, dammit hold your y'ead up
   And if thee's durst as much as answer 'm back they'd stick 'ee in the lock-up

4. Now they brought us in t'was dinner time, I was as hungry as [?] a hunter
   But I durst'nt touch or smell one bit, till the officer had been round sir
   They brought a dish, dished it up, on an old tin platter
   And all that I had when it come to my turn
   Was a bone and a blooming gurt tyater ["tater" = potato]

5. Lord don't I wish that I were back, a vollowin' our old plough sir
   Lord don't I wish that I were back, a milkin' our old cow sir
   Lord don't I wish that I were back, alongside a leg o' mutton
   With a damn gurt knife and a rusty old fork, ah lummee couldn't I cut 'en.

Source: Sung by David Gardner, Tresham, on 1st February 1997. Collected by Gwilym Davies

SINGERS AND THEIR SONGS

Singer/Musician	Songs and Tunes	Place
Albino, Henry Charles	Oh, Soldier Won't You Marry Me?	Bourton on the Water/Leicester/London
Allen, Henry	*Two dance tunes*	Ruardean/Gloucester
Ash, George	Here's Away to the Downs	Ampney Crucis
Avery, William	Leather Breeches Ploughman, The	Aldsworth
Baldwin, Charles	*Five dance tunes*	Newent
Baldwin, Stephen	Anyone Does For Me *and 58 dance tunes*	Newent
Ballinger, Tony	There was a Little Man There were Three Crows Swapping Song, The On a Four-masted Warship Barley Mow, The	Upton-St-Leonards
Bishop, Emily	Angel Gabriel, The Baffled Knight, The Banks of Sweet Primroses, Barbara Allen Christmas Now is Drawing Near At Hand Dark-Eyed Sailor, The Divers and Lazarus Fountain of Christ's Blood Here we Come a-Wassailing Jack Tar Line to Heaven, The Little Room, The Lord Lovel Moon Shines Bright, The	Bromsberrow Heath

	No Sir Northamptonshire Poacher, The On Christmas Night All Christians Sing Raggle Taggle Gypsies, The Virgin Unspotted, A	

Brazil, Danny	All For A Pretty Ploughboy
	Are We to Part like This, Bill?
	Ball of Yarn
	Banks of Sweet Dundee, The
	Betsy the Milkmaid (Blackberry
	   Fold)
	Bold Keeper
	Box on her Head
	Brandon on the Moor
	Come All You Lucky Gentlemen
	   (*Wassail*)
	Crabfish, The
	Croppy Boy/Macaffery
	Croppy Tailor, The
	Down by the Dark Arches
	   (Young Sailor Cut Down in his
	   Prime)
	Down in the Coalmines
	Game of all Fours, The
	Golden Glove, The
	Green Bushes
	Henry Martin
	Her Gown so Green
	I Met a White Maid
	If I Were a Blackbird
	Irish Sweep, The
	Jack and the Robber
	Limpy Jack (Thornymore
	   Woods)
	Lord Bateman
	Maria and Caroline (The
	   Folkestone Murder)
	Mossy Green Banks of the Lee,
	   The
	My Father is King of the
	   Gypsies
	My Love Willie (A Sailor's Life)
	Old Bog Road, The
	Old Man came Courting me, An
		Staverton

	Old Riverside, The
	Once a Bold Fisherman
	  Courted Me
	Out in Australia by the Setting
	  Sun (Sing me a Song of
	  Ireland)
	Poison in a Glass of Wine
	  (Jealousy/Oxford City)
	Poverty Street
	Rambling Irishman (Rambling
	  Journeyman)
	Resting on the Stile, Mary
	Rolling in the Dew
	Romany Rye
	Salisbury Ram (Derby Ram)
	Schoolmaster's Son, The
	Seamen Song, The (Cruel
	  Ship's Carpenter)
	Shake Hands and Be Brothers
	  again
	Shot Like a Bird on the Tree
	Side by Side (*parody*)
	Son Come Tell It Unto Me
	  (Edward)
	Song of the Thrush, The
	Three Brothers in Fair
	  Warwickshire
	Underneath her Apron
	
	Fragments:
	Brake of Briars
	Cuckoo, The
	Barley Straw, The
	Barbara Allen
	Freddie Archer	

Brazil, Harry	Blacksmith Courted Me Bold Keeper Green Bushes Green Grow the Laurels Pretty Ploughboy, The Long a-Growing Loyal Lover, The Through the Dark Arches	Gloucester

Brazil, Lemmie	Bitter Willow, The Green Bushes Irish Girl, The Little Sir Hugh Man You Don't Meet Every Day, The Pretty Ploughboy, The Shot Like a Bird on the Tree	Gloucester
Buckingham, Billy	Group Of Young Soldiers, A As I Came Home Come In The Parlour, Charlie Little Ball of Twine My Father's Name Was Adam Waysailing Bowl, The	Stonehouse
Carpenter, Robert	Pretty Ploughing Boy, The	Cerney Wick
Clayton, Mary Ann	Holly and the Ivy, The Long Looked For Come At Last Cherry Tree Carol Knight and the Shepherd's Daughter, The Orphan Boy, The Earl Richard Female Cabin Boy, The Green Bed, The Soldier's Boy, The	Chipping Campden
Clappem, Thomas	Unquiet Grave, The	Driffield
Clissold, Charlie	There Were Two Crows Ledbury Clergyman, The The Old Horse Died My Father was a Farmer *and several music hall songs*	Moreton Valence
Coldicott, Thomas	We Shepherds Are the Best of Men	Ebrington
Cook, Mrs	Robin Hood And The Widow's Three Sons	Quedgeley
Corbett, Henry	Irish Girl, The Cuckoo, The Lord Bateman Toby Derby Ram, The King George Shannon Side, The Shepherds Are The Best Of Men	Snowshill

Cross, Bob	Green Lived Upon The Green There Were Three Crows Young Sailor Cut Down In His Prime, The	Witcombe
Dibden, Albert	Wassail Song	Brockweir
Ellaway, Arthur	End of me Old Cigar Graveyard Song, The Somerset Fair	Charlton Kings
Evans, Joseph	Twelve Joys of Mary, The	Old Sodbury
Fletcher, Isabel and Mr.	Wife of Usher's Well, The King Herod and the Cock The Crafty Maid's Policy or I Met a Fair Damsel Holy Well, The	Cinderford
Gardner, David	Young Folk, Old Folk, Everybody Come They're Moving Grandad's Grave to Build a Sewer German Clockmaker, The Now Listen all you Sailor Boys Gloucester Blinder, The Varmer Giles	Tresham
Gill, Peter	Christ Came to Christmas Moon Shines Bright, The Dabbling in the Dew Shepherds are the Best of Men	Sheepscombe/ Stroud
Goode, Archer	British Soldier's Grave, The The Dunmow Flitch Guy Fawkes Jan's Courtship Jockey to the Fair Life of a Man, The Lost Lady Found, The Mistletoe Bough, The No, John No Seaweed Unquiet Grave, The	Charlton Kings/ Abergavenny/ Herefordshire
Hannis, Gwen	Your Baby has Gone down the Plughole Old Pine Tree, The Buttercup Joe	Cranham

Hannis, Reg	I'd Rather Lather Father than Father Lather me Seaweed Village Pump Buttercup Joe Gate Song Old Sow, The Father and the Cockadoodle-do Misery Farm Little Billy Williams Somerset Fair	Cranham
Hartland, Ray	Buttercup Joe Fisher's Boy, The Three Men went a-Travelling (a-Hunting) I wish I was Single Again Old Sow, The Pub with No Beer, The Twelve Stone Two song Ball of Yarn Billy Johnson's Ball My Husband's a Sailor	Eldersfield
Hawker, John	William Taylor	Broad Campden
Hawkins, Keziah	Twelve Joys of Mary, The	Old Sodbury
Hedges, William	Golden Vanity, The We Shepherds Are The Best Of Men Broken-hearted Gentleman, The Crafty Maid's Policy, The Fifty Long Miles Golden Vanity, The Horses to Grass I Followed Her John Ridler's Oven Pretty Nancy of Yarmouth Shepherds are the Best of Men Taffy Three Butchers, The *Tunes of*: Bold Fisherman, The Outlandish Knight, The Oxford City	Chipping Campden

	Rosemary Lane Three Butchers, The	
Hill, Beatrice	Annie Lee Lansdown Fair Little Pigs Londonderry Air, The Lord Lovel Maggie *and seven dance tunes*	Bromsberrow Heath
Hill, George Edward	A Bowl, A Bottle Tailor and the Carrion Crow, The	Dursley
Howman, Miss Jessie	Farmer's in the Dell May Garlands, The Poor Sally sits a-Weeping See the Robbers Coming Through Somersetshire Young Farmer's Son, A There was a Jolly Miller We Wish You a Merry Christmas	Stow on the Wold
Lanchbury, Thomas	Come Along with Me My Pretty Fair Maid Come Landlord Fill The Flowing Bowl Darling Miss Kitty Down in the Land of Greeno Farmer's Boy Good Old Geoff He's Gone To Rest Gossip Jones Jolly Shilling Stow Fair Up To Dick	Wyck Rissington
Lane, Archer	Twelve Apostles, The	Winchcombe
Lane, Ernie	Bandy Bertha Tram Song Big Strong Man My Wedding Day Cock-a-doodle-do Foggy Dew I'm Not All There Old Man came Courting Me, An	Teddington/ Dumbleton

	Hanging on the Old Barbed Wire Have a bit of Okey-Cokey I don' Work for a Living When You Wore a Tulip(Parody) Come for a Ride on my Tramcar I Bain't Half as Soft as I Looks I went to Market to Buy Me a Cow	
Lane, George (Daddy)	Banks of Sweet Dundee, The Claudy Banks High Germany Irish Girl, The Nightingale Sings, The Shepherd's Song Susan My Dear 'Twas Early, Early All In The Spring Valiant Munroe, The Wraggle Taggle Gypsies, The We Shepherds Are The Best Of Men	Alstone/ Winchcombe
Langsbury, Ken	Down in the Fields where the Buttercups all Grow Wing Wang Waddle-oh His Old Grey Head Kept Nodding	Cheltenham
Martin, William	Lost Lady Found Spotted Cow	Temple Guiting/ Winchcombe
Mason, John	Greensleeves Shepherdess, The *and at least 22 dance tunes*	Icomb/ Stow on the Wold
Newman, William	Farmer's Boy, The Saucy Sailor, The Where You Going To My Pretty Maid	Stanton
Newman, William	Outlandish Knight, The	Stanway
Packer, Mrs	Erin's Lovely Home Green Mossy Banks Of The Lee Lord Bateman Polly Oliver and The Three Gypsies	Stanton

	Mary And The Silvery Tide There Is An Alehouse	
Parsons, Dick	Waysailing Bowl, The Barley Mow, The German Clockmender, The Seven Joys of Mary, The Life of a Man, The	Shurdington

Partridge Family	Cherry Tree Carol, The
	Cock Fled Up in the Yew Tree,
	  The (*a version of I wish you a*
	  Merry Christmas)
	Shepherds of Old
	With Joy Awake
		Cinderford

Phelps, Charlie	John Barleycorn	Avening
Phelps, Sarah	Broomfield Hill, The Diamond Token, The Fox, The Outlandish Knight, The There Was an Old Woman Unquiet Grave, The	Avening
Protherough, Jerry	Buff Blow German Clockmender, The Thrashing Machine, The	Charlton Kings

Roberts, Mary
Anne
	Green Brooms
	[Bold] Fisherman, The
	Lord Lovel and Cherry Tree
	  Carol, The
	Today you may be Alive God
	  [sic] Man
	I Lived with my Grandmother
	Rich Bristol Squire, The
		Winchcombe

Shepherd, William (Daddy)	American Stranger Bold General Wolfe Brisk Sailor Lad Green Bushes Jolly Joe (The Collier's Son) My Love's Gone Saucy Jack Tar Seeds of Love Shepherd's Song Yonder Sits A Spanish Lady Young Fisherman, The Oh No John	Temple Guiting/ Winchcombe

	Joe the Pen Collier Who Knocks There We'll All Stand Up	

Smith, Wiggy	Macaffery
	Master Macgrath
	Bell Bottom Trousers
	Pretty Little Maiden
	Twenty-one Years
	Me Little Old Bedford
	Regiment of Soldiers, A
	Down by the Shannon Side
	The Ring Your Mother Wore
	Thorneycombe Woods
	Bloke You Don't Meet Every
	   Day
	Ikey Moses
	My Daddy Was Your Fireman
	Are We to Part Like This Bill
	Lord Bateman
	Romany Rai
	Twenty-one Years
	Auntie Maggie's Remedy
	I'll Take My Dog
	Little Old Band of Gold
	Cock Flew Up in the Yew-tree
	You're the Only Good Thing
	   that Has Happened to Me
	Barbara Allen
	Deserter, The
	Dunkirk Bay
	When Schooldays are Over
	Ikey Moses
	Rich Farmer of Sheffield
	Strawberry Roan
	Hobbling Off to the Workhouse
	   Door
	Riding Along in a Free Train
	High-low Well
	Cruel Ship's Carpenter
	Oakham Poachers, The
	Mandi Went to Puv the Grai
	When I Was a Young Man
	Mother's the Queen of My
	   Heart
		Elmstone
		Hardwicke

Smitherd, Elizabeth	Brisk Young Man, A
	As Jockey on a Summer's Morn
	Blow Away the Morning Dew
	Cuckoo, The
	Green Mossy Banks of the Lea
	In Shepherd Park
	It's of a Young Damsel
	Jack Williams, The Miser's
	   Daughter
	My Bonny Bonny Boy
	O Once I Courted a Fair Pretty
	   Maid
	Still Growing
	Orange and Blue, The
	Cruel Ship's Carpenter, The
	Our Captain Called All Hands
	Sailor and Beautiful Wife, A
	Unquiet Grave
	Poaching Song
		Tewkesbury

Tandy, Mr	Farmer's Lad, The Irish Girl, The Nancy Susan And Her Lovers There Was an Old Man (Green Broom)	Alderton/ Winchcombe
Teal, Mrs	Cold Blows The Wind Lord Lovell	Bishop's Cleeve/ Winchcombe
Toms (Tombs), Richard Thomas	Botany Bay Virgin Unspotted, A	Fairford/ Cirencester
Wakefield, Mr R.	Constant Farmer's Son, The	North Cerney/ Winchcombe
Wiggett, Mrs P.	Shepherdess, The Broken Token, The John Riley Blow The Fire Blacksmith Young Banker Jimmy and Nancy	Ford
Williams, Charley	Wassail Song While Shepherds Watched Black Degree, The Pilate's Rule Holly and the Ivy, The	

	Jacob's Well Our Saviour's Love	Brockweir
Williams, Claude	Wassail Song	Brockweir
Williams, Gilbert	Wassail Song	Brockweir

Williams, Kathleen	Barbara Ellen
	Bessie Watson or The Brisk
	   Young Lover
	Green Mossy Banks of the Lea
	Indian Lass, The
	Jock of Hazeldean
	Saddle My Horse
	T for Thomas
	When First to This Country a
	   Stranger
	Crab Fish, The
	Little Girl, The
	Fat Buck, The or Thorneymoor
	   Woods
	One Cow, The
	Still Growing
	Cuckoo, The
	I'm 17 Come Sunday
	Unquiet Grave, The
	White Cockade, The
		Mitcheldean/
		Drybrook

Wixey, Mrs	Geordie Rosetta Sailor Courted a Farmer's Daughter, A	Buckland

Appendix B

Places where the Singers Lived

Place	Singer/Musician	Songs and Tunes
Alderton/ Winchcombe	Tandy, Mr	Farmer's Lad, The Irish Girl, The Nancy Susan And Her Lovers There Was an Old Man (Green Broom)
Aldsworth	Avery, William	Leather Breeches The Ploughman, The
Alstone/ Winchcombe	Lane, George (Daddy)	Banks of Sweet Dundee, The Claudy Banks High Germany Irish Girl, The Nightingale Sings, The Shepherd's Song Susan My Dear 'Twas Early, Early All In The Spring Valiant Munroe, The Wraggle Taggle Gypsies, The We Shepherds Are The Best Of Men
Ampney Crucis	Ash, George	Here's Away to the Downs
Avening	Phelps, Charlie	John Barleycorn
Avening	Phelps, Sarah	Broomfield Hill, The Diamond Token, The Fox, The Outlandish Knight, The There Was an Old Woman Unquiet Grave, The

Bishop's Cleeve/ Winchcombe	Teal, Mrs	Cold Blows The Wind Lord Lovell
Bourton on the Water/ Leicester/ London	Albino, Henry Charles	Oh, Soldier Won't You Marry Me?
Broad Campden	Hawker, John	William Taylor
Brockweir	Dibden, Albert	Wassail Song
	Williams, Charley	Wassail Song While Shepherds Watched Black Degree, The Pilate's Rule Holly and The Ivy, The Jacob's Well Our Saviour's Love
Brockweir	Williams, Claude	Wassail Song
Brockweir	Williams, Gilbert	Wassail Song
Bromsberrow Heath	Bishop, Emily	Angel Gabriel, The Baffled Knight, The Banks of Sweet Primroses, The Barbara Allen Christmas Now is Drawing Near At Hand Dark-Eyed Sailor, The Divers and Lazarus Fountain of Christ's Blood Jack Tar Line to Heaven, The Little Room, The Lord Lovel Moon Shines Bright, The No Sir Northamptonshire Poacher, The On Christmas Night All Christians Sing Raggle Taggle Gypsies, The Virgin Unspotted, A Here we Come a-Wassailing

Bromsberrow Heath	Hill, Beatrice	Annie Lee Lansdown Fair Little Pigs Londonderry Air, The Lord Lovel Maggie *and seven dance tunes*
Buckland	Wixey, Mrs	Geordie Rosetta Sailor Courted a Farmer's Daughter, A
Cerney Wick	Carpenter, Robert	Pretty Ploughing Boy, The
Charlton Kings	Ellaway, Arthur	End of me Old Cigar Graveyard Song Somerset Fair, The
Charlton Kings	Protherough, Jerry	Buff Blow German Clockmender, Thrashing Machine, The
Charlton Kings/ Abergavenny/ Herefordshire	Goode, Archer	British Soldier's Grave, Dunmow Flitch, The Guy Fawkes Jan's Courtship Jockey to the Fair Life of a Man, The Lost Lady Found, The Mistletoe Bough, The No, John No, Seaweed Unquiet Grave, The
Cheltenham	Langsbury, Ken	Down in the Fields where the Wing Wang Waddle-oh His Old Grey Head Kept Nodding
Chipping Campden	Clayton, Mary Ann	Holly and the Long Looked For Come At Last Cherry Tree Carol, The Knight and the Shepherd's Daughter, The Orphan Boy, The Earl Richard Female Cabin Boy, The Green Bed , The Soldier's Boy, The

Chipping Campden	Hedges, William	Golden Vanity, The We Shepherds Are The Best Of Men Broken-hearted Gentleman, The Crafty Maid's Policy, The Fifty Long Miles Golden Vanity, The Horses to Grass I Followed her John Ridler's Oven Pretty Nancy of Yarmouth Shepherds are the Best of Men Taffy Three Butchers, The *Tunes of*: Bold Fisherman, The Outlandish Knight, The Oxford City Rosemary Lane Three Butchers, The
Cinderford	Fletcher, Isabel and Mr.	Wife of Usher's Well, The King Herod and the Cock Crafty Maid's Policy, The or I Met a Fair Damsel Holy Well, The
Cinderford	Partridge Family	Cherry Tree Carol, The Cock Fled Up in the Yew Tree, The (a version of I wish you a Merry Christmas) Shepherds of Old With Joy Awake
Cranham	Hannis, Gwen	Your Baby has Gone Down the Plughole Old Pine Tree, The Buttercup Joe
Cranham	Hannis, Reg	I'd Rather Lather Father than Father Lather me Seaweed Village Pump Buttercup Joe

		Gate Song Old Sow, The Father and the Cock-a-doodle-do Misery Farm Little Billy Williams Somerset Fair
Driffield	Clappem, Thomas	Unquiet Grave, The
Dursley	Hill, George Edward	A Bowl, A Bottle Tailor and the Carrion Crow, The
Ebrington	Coldicott, Thomas	We Shepherds Are the Best of Men
Eldersfield	Hartland, Ray	Buttercup Joe Fisher's Boy, The Three Men went a-Travelling (a-Hunting) I wish I was Single Again Old Sow, The Pub with No Beer, The Twelve Stone Two song Ball of Yarn Billy Johnson's Ball My Husband's a Sailor
Elmstone Hardwicke	Smith, Wiggy	Macaffery Master Macgrath Bell Bottom Trousers Pretty Little Maiden Twenty-one Years Me Little Old Bedford A Regiment of Soldiers Down By the Shannon Side The Ring Your Mother Wore, The Thorneycombe Woods Bloke You Don't Meet Every Day Ikey Moses My Daddy Was Your Fireman Are We to Part Like This Bill Lord Bateman Romany Rai Twenty-one Years Auntie Maggie's Remedy

		I'll Take My Dog Little Old Band of Gold Cock Flew Up in the Yew-tree You're the Only Good Thing that Has Happened to Me Barbara Allen Deserter, The Dunkirk Bay When Schooldays are Over Ikey Moses Rich Farmer of Sheffield Strawberry Roan Hobbling Off to the Workhouse Door Riding Along in a Free Train High-low Well Cruel Ship's Carpenter The Oakham Poachers Mandi Went to Puv the Grai When I Was a Young Man Mother's the Queen of My Heart
Fairford/ Cirencester	Toms (Tombs), Richard Thomas	Botany Bay A Virgin Unspotted
Ford	Wiggett, Mrs P.	Shepherdess, The Broken Token, The John Riley Blow The Fire Blacksmith Young Banker Jimmy and Nancy
Gloucester	Brazil, Harry	Blacksmith Courted Me Bold Keeper Green Bushes Green Grow the Laurels Pretty Ploughboy, The Long a-Growing Loyal Lover, The Through the Dark Arches

Gloucester	Brazil, Lemmie	Bitter Willow, The Green Bushes Irish Girl, The Little Sir Hugh Pretty Ploughboy, The Shot Like a Bird on the Tree The Man You Don't Meet Every Day
Icomb/ Stow on the Wold	Mason, John	Greensleeves Shepherdess, The *At least 22 dance tunes*
Mitcheldean/ Drybrook	Williams, Kathleen	Barbara Ellen Bessie Watson or The Brisk Young Lover Green Mossy Banks of the Lea Indian Lass, The Jock of Hazeldean Saddle My Horse T for Thomas When First to This Country a Stranger. Crab Fish, The Little Girl, The Fat Buck, The or Thorneymoor Woods One Cow, The Still Growing Cuckoo, The I'm 17 Come Sunday Unquiet Grave, The White Cockade, The
Moreton Valence	Clissold, Charlie	There Were Two Crows Ledbury Clergyman, The Old Horse Died, The My Father was a Farmer *and several music hall songs*
Newent	Baldwin, Charles	Five dance tunes
Newent	Baldwin, Stephen	Anyone Does For Me *58 dance tunes*

North Cerney/ Winchcombe	Wakefield, Mr R.	Constant Farmer's Son, The
Old Sodbury	Evans, Joseph	Twelve Joys of Mary, The
Old Sodbury	Hawkins, Keziah	Twelve Joys of Mary, The
Quedgeley	Cook, Mrs	Robin Hood And The Widow's Three Sons
Ruardean/ Gloucester	Allen, Henry	*Two dance tunes*
Sheepscombe/ Stroud	Gill, Peter	Christ Came to Christmas Moon Shines Bright, The Dabbling in the Dew Shepherds are the Best of Men
Shurdington	Parsons, Dick	Waysailing Bowl, The Barley Mow, The German Clockmender, The Seven Joys of Mary , The Life of a Man, The
Snowshill	Corbett, Henry	Irish Girl, The Cuckoo, The Lord Bateman Toby Derby Ram, The King George Shannon Side, The Shepherds Are The Best Of Men
Stanton	Newman, William	Farmer's Boy, The Saucy Sailor, The Where You Going To My Pretty Maid
Stanton	Packer, Mrs	Erin's Lovely Home Green Mossy Banks Of The Lee Lord Bateman Polly Oliver and The Three Gypsies. Mary And The Silvery Tide There Is An Alehouse
Stanway	Newman, William	Outlandish Knight, The

Staverton	Brazil, Danny	All For A Pretty Ploughboy
		Are We to Part Like This, Bill
		Ball of Yarn
		Banks of Sweet Dundee, The
		Betsy the Milkmaid (Blackberry Fold)
		Bold Keeper
		Box on her Head
		Brandon on the Moor
		Come All You Lucky Gentlemen (Wassail)
		Crabfish, The
		Croppy Boy/Macaffery
		Croppy Tailor, The
		Down by the Dark Arches (Young Sailor Cut Down in his Prime)
		Down in the Coalmines
		Game of all Fours, The
		Golden Glove, The
		Green Bushes
		Henry Martin
		Her Gown so Green
		I Met a Maid All in White
		If I were a Blackbird
		Irish Sweep, The
		Jack and the Robber
		Limpy Jack (Thornymore Woods)
		Lord Bateman
		Maria and Caroline (The Folkestone Murder)
		Mossy Green Banks of the Lee, The
		My Father is King of the Gypsies
		My Love Willie (A Sailor's Life)
		Old Bog Road, The
		Old Man came Courting me, An
		Old Riverside, The
		Once a Bold Fisherman Courted Me
		Out in Australia by the Setting Sun (Sing me a Song of Ireland)

		Poison in a Glass of Wine (Jealousy/Oxford City) Poverty Street Rambling Irishman (Rambling Journeyman) Resting on the Stile, Mary Rolling in the Dew Romany Rye Salisbury Ram (Derby Ram) Schoolmaster's Son, The Seamen Song, The (Cruel Ship's Carpenter) Shake Hands and Be Brothers again Shot Like a Bird on the Tree Side by Side (*parody*) Son Come Tell It Unto Me (Edward) Song of the Thrush, The Three Brothers in Fair Warwickshire Underneath her Apron *Fragments*: Brake of Briars Cuckoo, The Barley Straw, The Barbara Allen Freddie Archer
Stonehouse	Buckingham, Billy	Waysailing Bowl, The Come In The Parlour Charlie My Father's Name Was Adam Group Of Young Soldiers, A Little Ball of Twine As I Came Home
Stow on the Wold	Howman, Miss Jessie	Farmer's in the Dell, The May Garlands Poor Sally Sits a-Weeping See the Robbers Coming Through Somersetshire A Young Farmer's Son There was a Jolly Miller We Wish You a Merry Christmas

Stow on the Wold	Howman, Miss Jessie	Farmer's in the Dell, The May Garlands Poor Sally Sits a-Weeping See the Robbers Coming Through Somersetshire A Young Farmer's Son There was a Jolly Miller We Wish You a Merry Christmas
Teddington/ Dumbleton	Lane, Ernie	Bandy Bertha Tram Song Big Strong Man My Wedding Day Cock-a-doodle-do Foggy Dew I'm Not All There Old Man came Courting Me, An Hanging on the Old Barbed Wire Have a bit of Okey-Cokey I don' Work for a Living When You Wore a Tulip (Parody) Come for a Ride on my Tramcar I Bain't Half as Soft as I Looks I went to Market to Buy Me a Cow
Temple Guiting/ Winchcombe	Martin, William	Lost Lady Found Spotted Cow
Temple Guiting/ Winchcombe	Shepherd, William (Daddy)	American Stranger Bold General Wolfe Brisk Sailor Lad Green Bushes Jolly Joe (The Collier's Son) My Love's Gone Saucy Jack Tar Seeds of Love Shepherd's Song Yonder Sits A Spanish Lady Young Fisherman, The

		Oh No John Joe the Pen Collier Who Knocks There We'll All Stand Up
Temple Guiting/ Winchcombe	Shepherd, William (Daddy)	American Stranger Bold General Wolfe Brisk Sailor Lad Green Bushes Jolly Joe (The Collier's Son) My Love's Gone Saucy Jack Tar Seeds of Love Shepherd's Song Yonder Sits A Spanish Lady Young Fisherman, The Oh No John Joe the Pen Collier Who Knocks There We'll All Stand Up
Tewkesbury	Smitherd, Elizabeth	Brisk Young Man, A As Jockey on a Summer's Morn Blow Away the Morning Dew Cuckoo, The Green Mossy Banks of the Lea In Shepherd Park It's of a Young Damsel
		Jack Williams, The Miser's Daughter My Bonny Bonny Boy O Once I Courted a Fair Pretty Maid Still Growing, Orange and Blue, The Cruel Ship's Carpenter, The Our Captain Called All Hands A Sailor and Beautiful Wife. Unquiet Grave Poaching Song

Tresham	Gardner, David	Young Folk, Old Folk, Everybody Come They're Moving Grandad's Grave to Build a Sewer German Clockmaker, The Now Listen all you Sailor Boys Gloucester Blinder, The Varmer Giles
Upton-St-Leonards	Ballinger, Tony	Swapping Song, The There was a Little Man There were Three Crows Swapping Song, The On a Four-masted Warship Barley Mow, The
Winchcombe	Lane, Archer	Twelve Apostles, The
Winchcombe	Roberts, Mary Anne	Green Brooms [Bold] Fisherman, The Lord Lovel and Cherry Tree Carol, The Today you may be Alive God [sic] Man I Lived with my Grandmother Rich Bristol Squire, The
Witcombe	Cross, Bob	Green Lived Upon The Green There Were Three Crows Young Sailor Cut Down In His Prime, The
Wyck Rissington	Lanchbury, Thomas	Come Along with Me My Pretty Fair Maid Come Landlord Fill The Flowing Bowl Darling Miss Kitty Down in the Land of Greeno Farmer's Boy Good Old Geoff He's Gone To Rest Gossip Jones Jolly Shilling Stow Fair Up To Dick

ENDNOTES

1   *Field Notebooks /9 Book 5 1938-1952 original held at Sheffield University*

2   *Referenced in Roy Dommett's "Notes about the Sherborne Morris" Kennet Morris Men Workshops 1979/80.*

3   *Cecil J Sharp, The Morris Book. Part IV (London: Novello, 1911), 8-9.*

4   *Oxford Chronicle, 14 June 1856, 8*

5   *British History Online*

6   *A History of the County of Gloucester: Volume 6. Originally published by Victoria County History, London, 1965 published online by British History Online*

7   *source – the Forest Web*

8   *according to the Gwilliam Eergyng family tree on Ancestry.com*

9   *Thanks to the Forest Family History Society and the Gwilliam Eergyng family tree on Ancestry.com*

10 *Thanks to Philip Heath-Coleman for research on Stephen Baldwin*

11 *Further information on the Morris dance in the Forest of Dean can be found in the pamphlet 'The History of Morris Dancing in the Forest of Dean' by David Evans – see the Forest of Dean Morris Men.*

12 *Occupational categories are based on L Clarkson, The Pre-Industrial Economy in England, 1500-1700, 1971, pp 88-92*

13 *Village and Town: Occupations and Wealth in the Hinterland of Gloucester1660-1700 By PETER RIPLEY*

14 *Extract from Bartholomew's Gazetteer of the British Isles, 1887*

15 *www.glostradcom as of 18 March 2016*

16 *As well as these songs which Cecil Sharp collected from William Hedges, Hedges could only remember the tunes of the following songs: The Bold Fisherman, The Outlandish Knight, Oxford City, Rosemary Lane and The Three Butchers*

17 *Gloucestershire Archives Research Guide 15: Board of Guardians and Workhouse records November 2013*

18 *Fowler, Simon (2007), Workhouse: The People: The Places: The Life Behind Closed Doors, The National Archives, ISBN 978-1-905615-28-5*

19 *http://www.historyextra.com/workhouse)*

20 *Wilts and Gloucester Standard Thursday 6 September 2001*

21 *For further information on Eliza Wedgwood's song collecting see also 'Eliza Wedgwood and folk song collecting in Gloucestershire' article by Paul Burgess in Folk Song Conference 2013 EFDSS*

22 *Compiled by Peter Shepheard in 1968. My thanks also to Fred Chance and the Brazil family for the Brazil family photos*

23 *Thanks to Paul Pearson and Paul Burgess for information on Emily Bishop*

24 *Thanks to Richard Sermon for notes on Elizabeth Smitherd*

25 *Thanks to the contributors to the following family trees on Ancestry.com: bishop Family Tree, Stevens Family Tree, Pendleton May 2012, brown Family Tree, sheppard/workman, FRY 2010, Bate family tree, Pethybridge Family Tree.)*

26 *My thanks for the information on Beatrice Hill and Emily Bishop to the family of Beatrice Hill, Paul Pearson and Paul Burgess*

27 *Notes by Carol Davies with thanks to Ursula Groves-Smit*

28. *Also sung by Bob Cross at Brockworth, George Cook at Stow-on-the-Wold and as There Were Two Crows by Charlie Clissold at Moreton Valance.*

Carol Davies has been interested in the traditional music of Gloucestershire and family history research for many years. Together with her song collector husband, Gwilym, she has been a trustee and project manager of the national Lottery-funded project, the 'Single Gloucester' resulting in the setting up of the glostrad.com website, a wonderful source for the traditional songs and music of Gloucestershire. She has been a member of the folk groups Puzzlejug and the Green Willow band and leads the Shepherd's Crook Folk Choir. She is also interested in medieval and early Tudor music and sings and plays portative organ for the Waytes and Measures early music group. She has two adult children and lives in Gloucestershire.